A NO EXCEPTIONS NOVEL

the
Lover's
Game

J.C. REED

Cover art by Larissa Klein

Editing by Shannon Wolfman, Autumn Conley & Edee Fallon

ISBN: 1501032267
ISBN-13: 978-1501032264

To all who love and are loved:

Love grants us the power to forgive, to love when we're hurt, but it also gives us the courage to let go, and the understanding that to love, we love freely—at our own choice.

- J.C. Reed

I HOPE TO never see you again. Last time you betrayed me, I ran away. You looked for me and found me, and I chose to forgive you. This time, your secrets hit me much worse. I don't think I can ever recover. I don't think I can ever look at you and not be reminded of them. This time, I'll make sure you'll never find me.

I say that I hate you, but deep inside I love you. Love is in my mind, in my soul, and deep in my heart. As it always has been. As it always might be. But for how long? That I don't know. In love, we bonded. In passion, we rose. And in trust, we reconciled. I told myself that if you ever broke my heart again, karma would get back at you. And if it won't, if it takes too long, if it forgets, I will make sure revenge will pay you back.

My name is Brooke and I know this: Love has four letters.

One for you.

One for me.

One for our child.

One for revenge. Sweet, bitter revenge.

I bet you didn't see that one coming. I look forward to the day you'll feel the same pain I went through. I look forward to the day I can look at you in the knowledge that we're even. Maybe you had secrets, but this time I will make sure secrets won't be the only thing you carry home.

Chapter 1

The street was abuzz with life, the noise of traffic and human crowds droning in my ears. Tears trickled down my face in steady rivulets, as though my eyes were connected to an ocean. My legs carried me so fast that, at some point, my feet began to hurt, and I realized I had been running. And yet I didn't stop, not even when my lungs began to burn from the cold air and the lack of oxygen. It was only when I reached a bench in Central Park, the one where my sister and I used to sit ten years prior, that I stopped and slumped down, grateful for the cold, snow-covered wood that numbed my body.

He had broken me into pieces. The stupid fool I had been for falling in love with him, how could I have taken him back after he had betrayed me only to betray me again? And to think he told me I could trust him, that he loved me, that I was the only one in the whole world for him, and that he would never cheat on me.

Yeah, right!

They were stupid lies I had believed—lies I wanted to come true. Someone should have offered me a personality test and marked me "naïve, foolish," and let's not forget, "prone to being broke." When she had named me Brooke, my mother had apparently forgotten to remove the –o on my birth certificate, because now, I wasn't just broke in terms of money; I was also devoid of some much-needed wisdom—if only to see Jett for who he was when I had viewed him through rose-colored glasses: a cheater and lying bastard who was still seeing his ex behind my back. Sylvie had been right when she had warned me to be careful around him. I just wished she had shaken some sense into me rather than gushing about his good looks, all the while counterpointing that he was bad news, which was counterproductive. It hadn't exactly helped me ward off his advances; it only made me want him even more. His intensity had pushed me into a state of obsession, where desire became my addiction and hunger my passion. If it weren't for my longing to be loved, I never would have been so blind to his intentions.

I didn't know what hurt me more: the fact that I had

trusted him blindly—as in only seeing what I had wanted to see in him, trusting that he'd never lie or cheat on me. Or that he had actually done all the things he had promised he wouldn't do behind my back. And I hadn't even seen it coming because I had chosen to believe his promises.

Sexy men like him don't deserve another chance, another glance, another surrender. They deserve to have their ass kicked...and not only out of bed.

I couldn't wrap my mind around the fact that just a few hours earlier, I had been happy. Truly happy. There had been no warning, nothing to indicate that my life would be turned upside down. Even if I had wanted to, I couldn't have foreseen such events. There had been no signs to prepare me for what had happened or for all the feelings that had just crushed me to the core.

Minutes felt like hours. I didn't know how long I'd been sitting on the bench, oblivious to the people passing by and the curious glances they cast my way. But at some point, the cold began to creep up my body, intensifying the shudders running through me. I had never been so cold in my life, and yet I had never welcomed the numbing pain more than now. The cold did not only numb my limbs; it seemed to penetrate every layer of my being. But I had reached a point where I didn't care what happened to me, if I froze to death or if the world came to an end.

Everything had started out so well, and now I was, in so

many ways, back to square one: single, heartbroken, and broke—except I was a little worse off than before. In the beginning, I could have walked away from Jett in the hope that my heart would heal. I would have moved on to the next man who was eager to get into my panties, and I wouldn't have had to hide from shame.

But now I was pregnant, and while I had inherited the Lucazzone estate with all its dark secrets, that only added to the problems I couldn't run away from. With Nate free and on the loose, I still had to fear for my life. I had to give up on my dreams about a future with Jett.

Come to think of it, there was no sense in believing in an *us* anymore.

All that mattered now was keeping myself and my child safe, and the only way I could accomplish that was by getting far away from Jett and his family. But to accomplish that, I needed money. Even with my faith in men and in ever finding true love ripped to shreds, I could feel that my discovery was a blessing in disguise. The pain would be temporary, but in the end, the entire situation would serve a greater purpose because I finally knew which path to take.

I opened my handbag in search of the piece of the paper that was my beacon of hope. I had to give Thalia's job a try, because any job, as long as it paid the bills, was better than none. If only a tenth of Thalia's claims were true, then I had found a way to get away from here, from him, from everyone—a fresh start. Once everything calmed down, I'd focus on healing my heart and move on from a past that wasn't worth remembering.

Chapter 2

By the time she came, it was dark, and I had been waiting impatiently for almost an hour, my hands frozen in the pockets of my coat as I watched the late afternoon sun disappear. The beautiful Victorian-style lampposts were already switched on, their dull flicker casting an eerie yellow glow on the asphalted street. Central Park was magically beautiful, both during the day and at night. I usually avoided parks after dark, but today I was making an exception. To kill time as I waited for Thalia, I had walked around the southern half of the park. I had assumed it would be devoid of life at that hour, but to my surprise, clusters of people had gathered here and there, walking or jogging, immersed in their lives, probably struggling with their own demons.

After what seemed like an eternity, a car finally pulled over. From a distance, I spied Thalia getting out, right where we had arranged to meet. I waved to get her attention, then walked over.

Even under the weak illumination from the lampposts, I could see that the car was a scrambled mess with clutter all over the passenger and back seat. Never in my life had I met anyone so chaotic—except for Sylvie, when she was about to pack her suitcase and couldn't decide on what to take with her. It was as if Thalia had practically been living in her car; for all I knew, she had been.

"Jesus. What happened to you?" Thalia slammed the car door and turned to regard me. Her voice betrayed a worrying edge as she eyed me up and down. "Your lips are all blue, and you're freezing." She pulled my hands into hers and shivered as if to prove her point.

My tongue flicked over my numb lips. I hadn't realized my physical appearance would so easily give away the way I felt. Granted, I didn't have a mirror, so I had no clue how I looked. But surely it couldn't be that bad, apart from a bit of smudged mascara. I absent-mindedly smoothed my hair and smiled.

"It's not as bad as you think."

Deep worry lines creased her forehead, signaling that

she didn't believe me. "Do you want to talk about it?" she asked quietly, after a pause.

Great. Just great.

I figured I must really look like crap, which wasn't ideal, given the fact that I was supposed to go on a job interview. I should have changed at Sylvie's place. Or maybe not as, I thought, remembering why I'd decided against it in the first place: I couldn't deal with her questions, nor did I have the energy to recall all that had happened or, worse yet, acknowledge my mistakes and whatever hard facts I needed to accept.

"I'd rather not." Swallowing hard, I shot her a shy look. "I just had a crappy day, that's all."

"I don't mean to be pushy," Thalia said. "I've been told I'm a good listener, and I just want you to know I'm here to talk whenever you feel like it."

I shot her warm smile. "I appreciate that, but I'm not ready. Sorry. Maybe another time?"

"All right." She eyed me one last time before she sighed. "I brought coffee. Figured you might want one." She inclined her head toward the car, signaling that she was about to change the subject. "Sorry I kept you waiting. I had to clean the floor after my shift."

"No problem. I'm just really grateful you're offering to take me along."

"You really need this job, huh?" Thalia pointed around

the car impatiently, a sign that she wanted to leave. I walked around and slid into the passenger seat.

"After today, I definitely do," I said, realizing there was no point in lying.

I watched her walk around to her side and hop into the driver's seat. Leaning forward, she handed me a cup of coffee.

"Thank you."

I warmed my cold hands against the cup containing the hot liquid, then took a tentative sip. After being outside in the cold for hours, the warmth soothed me from the inside, and I savored the flavor of coffee, sugar, and whipped cream, reminding me that I was still alive and living.

"Don't worry. I'll persuade Grayson to give you a job, but first—" Her eyes brushed over my clothes in thought before she pointed to the cluttered mess on her back seat, "—we need to get you out of that. I have countless dresses I bought before my self-imposed shopping ban. There should be one that fits you. My motto is, 'If you look good, you feel good.' So…" She shrugged and paused, hesitation written all over her face, as though she wasn't sure why she was about to divulge such information "Whenever I have a bad day, I dress up. It makes the world a better place, at least for a while."

At that moment, Thalia officially sounded like Sylvie. I decided to like her; after all, anyone who resembled my friend Sylvie had to be a good person. In fact, I figured most human beings on the planet were better than Jett and his sick family. Compared to them, Thalia was a God-sent angel, and through her, for the first time in my life, I saw a way out, a way to escape my debts.

"I don't know why you're doing it, but thank you for helping," I whispered.

Staring out the car window, various emotions washed over me as thoughts kept spinning in my mind. The job was an option. An option I could accept, but didn't have to. Still, the more I thought back to my college days, eating ramen noodles day in and day out, working my ass off to avoid amassing a fortune in loans, the more I was convinced I was doing the right thing. And I really didn't care what I had to do, as long as I was in control of my own life. And control I was seeking.

Finally, there was a light at the end of the tunnel, an escape from a precarious financial situation that I had thought would keep me enchained for the rest of my life. My best friend had always told me that if I wanted something, I had to work hard to achieve it. I had done that, but as it turned out, working hard was not enough, and it was certainly not always the fastest way to solve a problem. So I had always poured everything I had into my career, but now, a shortcut was necessary.

Taking this job could be my shortcut. I was willing to

adapt, to change, to try something new, and to take on challenges I hadn't faced before.

Whatever it takes. It was time to write my own destiny.

As silently as I could, I switched off my cell phone, so no one could reach me.

Chapter 3

The streets were busier than usual, and the car seemed to stop at every corner. We had been driving for at least forty minutes when we finally reached an area close to the Williamsburg Bridge. The car came to a screeching halt in front of a red, three-story building, and I got out. From the outside, in the dark, it seemed rather ordinary, if not even a bit run-down. If I hadn't known any better, I wouldn't have had a clue that it was actually the studio of a successful photographer slash artist. There was certainly no sign indicating the opportunity of a promising job.

A cold wind whipped my hair into my face, and I wrapped my coat tighter around me. Shivering near the entrance, I watched Thalia change her sneakers for a pair of high heels. She tossed the athletic shoes onto the back seat and retrieved an oversized training bag, which I assumed contained her outfit for the job.

"Is he famous?" I asked as she locked up the car.

"Who?"

"Grayson."

"I wouldn't say that, but he is well established and known for his exquisite taste and expensive art collection." She turned to shoot me a strange look, then glanced up at the windows. "Whatever he shows you, keep any remarks to yourself. His art takes a while to get used to, if you ask me, but he takes it very personally when someone doesn't like it."

"Is it that bad?"

She laughed. "See for yourself. As they say, beauty is in the eye of the beholder. I've never understood his taste, but I'm not exactly a creative genius. Maybe it'll appeal to you. Who knows?"

She slung the bag over her shoulder and let herself in, motioning for me to follow her up a narrow staircase. Her cryptic words had left me eager to find out what she had meant by "exquisite taste." Was this Grayson renowned for his taste in selecting just the right model for the job, or did his art cater to the strange and bizarre? The countless questions floating in my mind kept me intrigued and focused and not just as a distraction that helped me forget my relationship drama. As far as impressions went, Grayson was a big, blurry question mark. I knew next to nothing about him, and the sudden realization of the unknown made me nervous.

"What happens with the pictures he takes?" I asked. "Does he always sell them?"

"Usually, yeah." Thalia nodded slowly. "Most go to rich collectors, fans of the fifties era. Others he sells to magazines and film and music studios. He keeps only a few for himself. This is the place where he usually hangs out when he's not traveling. Sometimes he rents out his studio to art events, gallery shows, and launch parties, which is how he raises his profile. Before he became a photographer, he owned a modeling agency."

She pressed a button above a polished steel plate that had "GR Photography" engraved on it. Within seconds, the door buzzed and opened. We stepped into a large hall decorated with marble pillars, huge mirrors, and hardwood flooring. In some ways, it reminded me of an art gallery with white naked walls and high ceilings. No flowers, no paintings adorning the walls.

"This is the waiting area," Thalia explained in a muted voice.

I nodded as I let my gaze sweep over the plain white leather couches and matching chairs near an unoccupied glass reception desk set up in the middle of the room.

"Obviously, Grayson's expecting us, so we're not going to wait here," Thalia continued and pointed at a door marked "Studio."

As we passed the reception desk and crossed the corridor, my eyes fell on a life-sized sculpture. Just looking at it gave me the creeps and yet I stepped back to analyze it, unable to peel my eyes off the horrid statue. It took me a few seconds to process what I was seeing. The thing was carved from wood and reminded me of a distorted face with an open mouth and big, alien eyes reflecting terror. The body resembled a deformed man surrounded by blazing fire, his arms waving as though to cry for help, while his feet were rooted in what looked like earth. I shuddered at just how ugly it was. Actually, ugly was an understatement. It was dreadful. In one word: monstrous. So bad it was almost funny. I pressed my hand over my mouth to suppress a giggle. It was so deplorable and grotesque that I was surprised Grayson's visitors weren't too freaked out to return.

"What the hell is this?" I whispered. "If I had something like this in my home, I wouldn't be able to close my eyes at night."

Thalia laughed quietly in my ear. "He calls it his 'mandrake.' Scary as shit. Now, that's the art I was talking about. He is kind of obsessed with it." She pulled at my arm gently. "Like I said, pop over a few times, and you won't even notice it anymore. But if he asks, tell him you love it."

I nodded and Thalia led me through yet another door into a well-lit space with floor-to-ceiling mirrors and various places to sit.

"This is the dressing room."

Compared to the entrance hall, this room felt oppressing and tight. Maybe it wasn't the lack of space as much as the fact that it was littered with clothes and carrier bags, and shoes strewn across the floor.

"From the sight of it, Grayson's busy." Thalia pointed to the ceiling.

I was just about to point out that I had no idea what she was talking about when soft thudding sounds carried down from above. People rushing around. Jumping. Perhaps even dancing.

Moving past the mirrors, I caught my reflection and winced. My hair looked presentable enough. Being curly and wavy, it never needed a brush. But my face was a mess: my skin pale from exhaustion, the bags under my eyes swollen and dark. There was no doubt I looked as though I had attended a funeral. I laughed inwardly at my morbid thoughts. It some way, I *had* been at one. While sitting in Central Park, I had mourned my old self and all those things I'd never have: a family with Jett, a father for my child.

Thalia glanced at her watch.

"We're late. We have to hurry." She retrieved a blue *Donna Morgan* print dress from her bag and pushed it into my hands. "Try this on. It should fit you."

I changed quickly, aware of her eyes on me, and then followed her silent command to sit down when she pointed to a chair. Her hands immediately began to busy themselves with my hair and makeup. My curls were pulled up and twisted with bobby pins, then, with a precision and ease I had never possessed, Thalia started to transform my face into flawlessness, complete with porcelain skin and huge, hazel eyes, framed by dark green eyeliner. She paused to inspect her work before resuming with the confidence of a professional artist.

"Where did you learn to do this?" I asked.

"I'm self-taught," she said with justified pride. "As a teen, I wanted to be a makeup artist, so I used to spend my time reading fashion magazines and blogs. Even though I couldn't afford school, the knowledge has come in handy." She applied a touch of mascara and stepped back to regard me, apparently satisfied with the result. "There you go! You have stunning eyes. You should wear more green and gray."

"Thank you."

She pointed at the mirror and began to put away her brushes.

For a moment I hesitated, afraid of what I might see.

Taking a deep breath, I lifted my gaze and almost didn't recognize myself. "Wow. You're good." I stared at myself, unable to look away. "Really good." And I meant every bit of praise.

The woman standing in front of me didn't look like Brooke Stewart at all. She didn't look hurt and broken. She looked confident and sexy.

The kind of woman no one would ever dare to cheat on.

Self-doubt passed over me. What if I had never really been sexy enough for Jett? What if my insecurities and my inability to trust him completely had pushed him away? Maybe he had missed the excitement and the confidence women of his social status often exuded. Maybe he started cheating on me because I wasn't like them?

I turned back to Thalia, glad she didn't seem to notice the sudden drop in my mood, and watched her change into a peach-colored dress with fishnet stockings. I had to admit, not only did she have a gorgeous body with toned legs and hips to die for, but the attire seemed to be her thing, as though she never wore anything else.

"Do you like your job?" I resumed the conversation as she began to paint her lips a bright shade of red.

"I do." She nodded, and with a glance in the mirror she smacked her lips. "I'm a big fan of anything burlesque because it's so feminine. You snap a picture, and you can be sure it's going to be perfect. There's nothing ugly about being a pin-up girl, Jenna."

I flinched at hearing the sound of my sister's name, and realized I had forgotten that I had adopted a false identity. Oblivious to my reaction, Thalia began to apply some of her lipstick on my lips and then snapped the cap shut. "What we are doing is nothing to be ashamed of. It's not porn, but art, and that makes all the difference."

She flashed me a smile, revealing two beautiful rows of pearly white teeth and slight dimples that gave her character. "The way I see it, it's an honor," she continued, her hazel eyes regarding me warmly, "to help a man dream of his perfect girl—one who's out of his reach. We're what I'd call a fantasy, a dream, something most men will never have." She grabbed my hand, infusing some chirpiness in her voice. "Come on. Time to meet Grayson."

Chapter 4

By the time we returned to the hall and ascended a staircase, I was beginning to think it was all a mistake. My heart was pounding so hard I could feel the blood rushing in my ears, threatening to burst my veins. What had I been thinking? I didn't have Thalia's confidence. I didn't have her gorgeous looks. In no way would I be suitable for working as a model. I could call myself lucky if this Grayson guy didn't laugh. I was better off finding a job in real estate and waiting tables in the evening.

Don't be stupid, Stewart. You can't afford to live off just one income, and topping it off with tips certainly wouldn't make a difference.

My heart sank in my chest as I realized that not only did I need a second job, but if I was to avoid Jett for the rest of his life, I'd have to stop working for him. That meant I'd have to look for a new job, all without health insurance and probably no references. And then there was the matter of my ever-growing loan problems.

Ninety thousand dollars debt!

I still had trouble wrapping my head around that part.

You'll be repaying loans for the rest of your life, Stewart. That is, unless you start taking risks.

And this was indeed a risk, not just for my finances, but also for my confidence.

Confidence or not, I had no choice but to go through with the interview. If I didn't try, I might end up living in a small, rented apartment forever, with no opportunity to offer my child the best life he or she could possibly have.

"There's nothing to be afraid of." Thalia's voice, meant to reassure, only managed to make me more nervous.

"I know." I sighed, biting my thumbnail.

We took a left turn through yet another corridor and entered a door that led into a large hall. Pretty girls stood in clusters, waiting. Some were talking on their cell phones; some were sitting on the floor, all dressed in peach-colored, knee-length burlesque dresses and black high heels. For a waiting area, it was surprisingly silent.

Thalia waved to a few, then headed straight for a door

and knocked. When a male voice called out, ordering her to enter, Thalia mouthed, "Wait here," and slipped inside, then closed the door behind her. I pressed my back against the wall and tried hard not to overhear the hushed voices carrying through from inside. The seconds stretched into minutes. Finally, the door opened again and Thalia returned, looking slightly flushed.

"He's waiting for you," she whispered to me. "Good luck."

I watched her join the other women, a part of me hoping someone would go in with me.

Get a grip, Stewart. You're an adult. There's nothing to be scared of.

Taking a deep breath, I started to count backwards.

Three.

Two.

One.

The door flew open, and I stepped back in shock.

"Aren't you coming in?" he asked, knitting his eyebrows together.

I had been so immersed in my thoughts and worries that I had left my potential future boss waiting. For a moment, I stared into his eyes.

Holy cow.

Another arrogant guy.

Could my day get any worse?

I sounded bitter in my thoughts, I realized, already hating the whole male population when dating would soon become a perquisite—even a necessity—to distract me and help get me over my feelings for Jett.

"Sorry," I muttered and rushed in, closing the door behind me.

"You still want to do the interview, right?" Grayson turned to regard me with an amused expression.

I stared at him, perplexed. "Yeah. Of course I do."

Even though he was the owner of GR Photography and, according to Thalia, had been successful for a number of years, he didn't look much older than thirty. His dirty blond hair was cropped short and messy in a sexy way, and he was dressed in jeans and a dark blue polo T-shirt that fit his tan body. Unlike Jett, he wasn't all muscles and dark hair and green eyes, but he compensated in height. His blue eyes and scruffy beard gave him a stylish rock-star appearance and made him look rugged and masculine—and absolutely not the way I had envisioned him.

What the heck are you doing comparing this guy to Jett?

I groaned inwardly. At the rate I was going, I'd never get over Jett.

Never.

Because, apparently, I couldn't stop fawning over Jett's pair of sinfully sexy eyes and the kind of body that keeps you hot and sweaty at night.

Focus, Stewart. Focus. First, the job interview. Then the self-loathing.

His brows shot up. "Well?"

Damn.

Had I been so absorbed that I didn't notice he had been waiting for me to introduce myself? Suppressing the urge to turn on my heels and run out the door to get back to my dark thoughts and dwell in the aftermath of the recent discoveries, I cleared my throat.

"Yes. I'm Br—" I took a deep breath, realizing my mistake. "Jenna."

He shook my extended hand and sat down at his desk.

"Please take a seat." He pointed to a chair that faced his desk and his blue eyes began to measure me up and down with the air of a professional.

I forced my legs to move, though all I managed was to stumble forward and plop into the chair with the grace of a grizzly bear. "Thank you."

I swallowed past the lump in my throat as I settled into the chair. His penetrating presence did nothing to calm down the frantic beating of my heart. Now I knew why I had never liked job interviews: They always made you feel inferior, as if I had messed up and had just been given a tiny chance to prove in less than ten seconds that I was worth the hassle. Smiling at Grayson, I realized this felt even worse because I wasn't just applying for any job. I also had to prove I had what it took in the looks and sex appeal department while, under Grayson's scrutinizing eyes, I felt completely exposed—even more so because, even though he was a bit too lean for my taste, he was still good-looking.

I expected him to sit back and start the usual interrogation, but he stood and walked around the desk, then stopped just inches away from me, his leg almost brushing mine in the process.

"All right." He sighed and folded his arms over his chest as he leaned back against the desk. "So… Jenna, right?"

I nodded.

"Thalia tells me you're interested in working for me. Have you modeled before?"

"No." I forced the word past my lips in a hesitant huff. I had expected the question, but not straight away, and it unsettled me. "I don't have any experience in modeling at all."

"It's okay," Grayson said, as though reading my mind. "A lot of girls start here with nil experience. I like to see them as diamonds in the rough that only have to be cut and polished into priceless gems."

Wow. No modesty there.

For some reason, the analogy made him instantly likeable. I smiled, and he pushed a clipboard toward me, inclining his head in the process, silently urging me to take a look. I peered at the questionnaire and then back at him.

"Let's start with a few basic questions to see if you're suitable for the job," Grayson said.

"Great." I watched him unscrew the lid of his pen and grab the clipboard out of my hand.

"Full name?"

"Jenna Stewart," I said carefully.

"Age?"

"Twenty-three."

"Status?"

I stared at him, but it wasn't him I was seeing; rather, it was the image of Jett kissing Tiffany, her arms around him, her body pressed against his. I wondered if he had slept with her after that kiss. Probably. That led to the next question: How often had they met behind my back? Jett had had plenty of opportunities to see her all those times when he had pretended to work late while I was stuck at home, clueless and under the impression he really loved me.

"Status?" Grayson repeated and slowly looked up from his clipboard, his blue eyes piercing through me with such an intensity that it felt like a breeze was touching my soul.

Status? Stupid.

Apparently, I had failed at yet another relationship and it was all my fault. Some things about human evolution never changed, and that included hard-to-get players like Jett and morons like me, who were quick to love and even quicker to lose. The whole time I had been with Jett, I had been under the impression he would surmount his urge to be free and settle down with me, maybe even get married. I had pictured it all—the white fence, the nursery, we as a family sitting at the dinner table—all the while forgetting the most important fact: Jett didn't believe in rules, restrictions, and boundaries.

"Single," I said, because I couldn't share my true thoughts. My voice sounded choked, but Grayson didn't seem to notice.

"Good." He nodded. "One of the secrets to success is no distractions whatsoever. Nothing that interferes with the job."

I laughed bitterly. "Yeah, that's so true."

And it was. If I had never been in love with Jett, I would have been more focused. I would have known that something was wrong with him and our relationship as a whole.

"Any health problems or conditions I should know of?"

Sighing, I fiddled with the hem of the dress. This was the perfect time to tell him about the pregnancy, but I decided against it. First of all, it was none of his business. Second, he might decide it was a distraction. Third, he could have very well been one of those men who thought pregnancy was something ugly, and I couldn't afford another blow to my ego.

I shook my head and replied, "None that I know of."

"Height and weight?"

I answered his questions patiently. At last, after what seemed like an eternity, he put the clipboard away, signaling that he was about to finish his interrogation, and retrieved a measuring tape from one of the drawers.

"Bra size?"

I stared at him, then moistened my lips, uncomfortable with the inquiry.

He noticed my reaction. "It's for my clients," he explained.

"I know. Sorry."

I swallowed the lump in my throat and answered his question, and then he motioned for me to stand, the measuring tape dangling from his hand.

Surely, he wasn't going to…A shiver moved through me at the thought of him touching me or expecting me to undress. Until recently, it had never occurred to me that any man other than Jett would ever roam his hands over my body. Granted, it was never intended to be a sexual situation, but it still felt intimate. Unexpected. Strange. And I was still bleeding from Jett's betrayal. I wouldn't have been surprised to look under my clothes and find my body broken, bloody, and shattered for the whole world to see.

"Do you mind if I take your measurements?" Grayson asked. "My clients are very specific."

Actually, I did care, but I could hardly refuse—not when

he was kind enough to ask.

Shaking my head with trepidation, I said, "Of course not."

He motioned for me to stand up again, and this time I did as he expected of me. I held my breath as his hand went around my waist gently. He stopped in midair, his face mere inches away from mine as he looked at me amused.

"You don't have to hold your breath, Jenna."

With my gaze glued to the floor, I forced my breath out. He was standing so close, I was sure he could feel the nervous pounding of my heart. I could feel his hot breath on my skin and, for some reason, it felt odd and slightly unsettling. Almost forbidden, as if no other man should be allowed to touch me after Jett.

"Why do you want this job?" he asked gently as he continued to measure me: first my hips, then my waist, his hand close to my skin without really touching me. I figured it was a means to divert my attention and make me feel more comfortable. To my surprise, it worked because, gradually, I began to relax. Maybe because deep down I knew he was a professional and probably used to touching all types of women, used to beauty, perfection, and human flaws.

"I have debts," I heard myself say even though I had no idea why I was being so honest.

"How much do you owe?"

His candidness startled me. I stared at him, surprised at the fact that I wanted to confide in him. "Almost a hundred grand."

His blue gaze pierced me, but there was no judgment in his eyes. "That's a lot."

I nodded and took a long breath, then let it out slowly. "I know."

For a moment, we remained quiet. Our eyes connected and my heart began to thump just a little bit harder—not because I wanted him, but because he seemed to understand. His measuring tape was around my shoulder, and for a moment, the unwelcome image of him kissing me popped into my mind, and how much that would hurt Jett. How much that would give *me* the satisfaction of knowing I might actually be able to hurt him as much as he had hurt me. But that wasn't me. I couldn't stoop so low. Besides, I knew I wouldn't be able to deal with the shame and self-loathing.

Heat began to pour through me, not from sexual attraction but from the disturbing thoughts I harbored about my possible future boss. As if sensing my sudden shame, Grayson broke our eye contact.

"There was a time when I owed $400,000," he said and removed the tape, his voice quiet.

"Four?"

He nodded. "I was a struggling artist and photographer

for ages, working on commission, waiting to be picked for jobs from among incredible competition, all while drowning in debt."

"What happened?" I asked when he fell silent. He had shown interest in my problems, and it was only natural to inquire about his. I had sensed the moment I saw those girls talking that they had a good working relationship with him, and I had been right.

Grayson leaned back against the desk and began to rub his chin as he exhaled slowly, his eyes reminiscent of the past. "I figured I could either continue on that path that would eventually lead to complete self-destruction and self-hatred, or I could do something about it. There weren't many options left." He looked up again, his eyes sparkling with defiance. "I borrowed more money and started my own business, focusing on finding diamonds in the rough while relying on rich benefactors, working on appearance. I poured all the money I earned into advertising and hosting parties, building connections, until I found one rich investor who helped me put together a client list, one at a time." He smiled, his face relaxing slightly. "I worked my ass off day and night, but taking out a bigger loan was a risk worth taking. To make a business successful, you have to invest in it." His pale blue eyes assessed me, and his lips twitched, though whether it was with amusement or sarcasm I couldn't tell. "What? You thought it was all *given* to me?"

I hesitated. Considering that Grayson was so young, I actually had thought so, but I wasn't going to admit that to him. Instead, I said, "Surely it must have cost a fortune to set up a studio and build a reputation."

He rolled up the measuring tape and jotted the numbers down, taking his time to answer. "It wasn't cheap, and there were times when I doubted my decision."

"Why?"

Grayson hesitated again, as though he was unsure as to whether or not to reveal the truth. "I'm a school dropout. My family was poor, so I had no other choice than to start working. Everything I've built is the result of my struggles and learning from mistakes—lots and lots of mistakes, by me and others." He turned to me, narrowing his eyes in thought. "The most important thing I've learned along the way is that it's okay to quit when something isn't working out, because continuing is a waste of my time and energy. You have to put faith in your abilities. Most people make the mistake of focusing on too many things at a time, making too many plans that are impossible to follow through on. I focused on what I was good at and listened to people's wishes and demands." He put the measuring tape away and returned with a camera. "You know what I always say to young artists who ask me for advice?"

I shook my head because I had no idea.

"Hope is the nightingale that still sings while the night is young. It's my favorite quote, a reminder that a bad situation, a bad experience, should never stop you from having faith. Eventually, you'll find the right path."

He pointed to the white wall, and I walked over, waiting for instructions. From the corner of my eyes, I scanned the far side of the wall, which was covered with pictures of beautiful models, some in lingerie, others wearing clothes. Even among so many beautiful faces, Thalia stood out straight away.

I almost flinched when Grayson touched my chin with surprisingly warm fingers. My skin started to tingle as he gently turned my face to the right, then down.

"Perfect," he muttered and stepped back. A flash blinded me, and within seconds, a Polaroid photo emerged. He waved it in the air until the white space turned into a colored image of my face. He wrote my fake name on the picture and attached it to the questionnaire with a clip.

"We're done. You can sit down." With the file in his hand, he walked over to his desk and slumped into his seat.

"Will you give me a chance?" I asked after a pause.

He began to tap his pen against his lips. I tried to read his expression, but his eyes remained expressionless. Eventually he said, "It depends." He leaned back with an expression I couldn't decipher. "Will you go nude?"

I stared at him, perplexed. All the positive thoughts I

had harbored about him, were now gone, disappearing like bubbles in the air.

"Thalia said I wouldn't have to take off my clothes."

"That's true." He nodded, and for the first time, he genuinely smiled as though something amused him. "But there's this thing with your height."

What the heck was wrong with my height—or the lack thereof?

I frowned, unsure where the conversation was heading.

"What's wrong with it?" I asked.

"I'll be honest with you, Jenna. You have good proportions, though not model perfect, and a good face, which I'm sure will appeal to some of my clients," Grayson continued, "but you're a few inches too short to work as a model."

My temper flared.

"I'm as tall as Thalia." I jutted my chin out.

He smiled again, then moved over to me and leaned against the desk again, regarding me coolly. "That might be true, but Thalia's exotic. Her heritage, part Creole/American and Indian/Italian, is very popular with my clients, so she's in high demand. You, in turn...I don't know how to put this nicely...you're common."

Ouch.

Enough insults for a day. It had been a bad idea to come. Obviously, I was wasting my time.

"You might as well have told me straight away that I'm fit for the job before you wasted my time and yours with all those questions," I said.

Holding my head high, I stood up and headed for the door. Grayson's fingers curled around my upper arm, stopping me in my tracks. "I'm not finished."

I snapped my head back in annoyance, and Grayson let go of my arm. As he caught my glance, his smile vanished, and he returned to his previous reserved self.

"I never said you aren't a good fit," he said quietly. "The job is yours, as long as you're willing to go along with my clients' demands, and go nude."

I would never pose nude. Never. The thought was *absurd*. "What if I don't agree with something they want?"

He shrugged. "Then you won't get the job. Given your situation, if you want to earn good money, nude shoots are exactly what you need. Flexibility and the willingness to go nude is how I secure a working contract with a client, not just for a single job but for future work as well. If a client likes working with a particular model, they'll want to book her again."

"I work with clients, and am aware of the importance of customer satisfaction," I remarked dryly. I certainly didn't need a lecture on that. Sighing, I leaned back and crossed my arms.

He wet his lips carefully in thought, his glance moving

from my eyes to my lips, and for an instant, I felt another pang of shame burning through me.

"Look, all I'm saying is that I need you to be flexible." He spread his hands out. "Your options are limited, not least because you're not exactly the right height. So, the only option is to offer them more, including a great personality and a little bit of skin." He paused to take in my reaction. When I remained quiet, he continued. "I'm not saying you absolutely *have* to go nude. I'm also not saying you'll have to go nude for every single work contract. All I'm saying is that you should keep the option open rather than being so judgmental about it, because I have many different clients with many different needs."

He was probably right, but I wasn't convinced just yet. "How do you define *nude*?" I asked.

He leaned forward, so close I could see the little flecks in his blue iris. "Nude can mean a lot of things, Jenna. It can be topless, bikini, or panty. It can even be implied nude, where you cover certain body parts. Many of my clients want that. In this kind of job, as long as you are willing to go nude, you can choose the limit, what you are comfortable with, but some of my clients want to see skin."

I shook my head. "I don't want to be topless, even if I can cover up," I explained.

"I understand." He leaned back again and regarded me with an expression I couldn't place.

For a moment, silence ensued between us.

Awkward silence.

His expression showed hesitation, as though he was considering whether I was really worth the trouble. Or maybe he thought I was an idiot for not taking him up on his offer when he was generous enough to give me a chance. Suddenly, I was reminded of the fact that I was pregnant and had no money. Terrified that I might not find another well-paying job anytime soon. After college, I had been unemployed for nine months, only to land a poor-paying job. What if I had to wait another nine months to secure my next position? Besides, who would hire a mother-to-be with a child on the way?

This pregnancy would change my body, and not for the better. What if there was no job at all for me in the near future, unless I agreed to taking off my clothes or…worse?

My God.

My heart slumped in my chest.

As much as I hated the idea of being half-nude or naked, I figured I tolerate it for the time being—as long as I could use my arms and hands to cover up and I still had the confidence, no stretch marks, good skin, and felt more or less human, without the urge to throw up or pee.

"You know, those strict morals won't get you far in this industry," Grayson remarked. "I did worse to build up my career and get it going. The girls you saw out there use their jobs as a backup, to get started."

What the heck did he mean by "strict morals?" Was it such a bad thing that I preferred not to show my private business to the entire world? I swallowed the lump in my throat, suddenly afraid that Grayson might find me too difficult to work with, that he had the impression I was too proud.

"As long as I'm not butt naked, I'll be okay with it," I said and raised my head defiantly. "Obviously, I prefer clothes, but if there are really no other options, then I'll do it. But I won't do more than that, and it has to be tasteful and classy at all times." I was about to add, "Take it or leave it," then decided against it. He seemed like a nice guy; there was no need to alienate or insult him and his line of work.

Grayson unscrewed his pen and scribbled something on the paper. Eventually, he dropped his pen on the desk and crossed his ankles in front of him, staring at the floor.

"Jenna, it's not about me. It's about them—my clients." He sighed. "This is a supply-and-demand business, and my clientele can be very specific in their demands. They often come to me with certain expectations and demand that my models follow through with them. No exceptions. I can't afford to hire models who refuse to comply with the requests. It would be bad for my reputation, not to mention unprofessional. Do you understand?"

"I understand, however—" Leaving the rest unspoken, I

drew a sharp breath, ready to stand my ground. "So where does this leave me?"

Grayson clasped his hands together and began to tap his thumbs in thought. "What I can do for you is add you to our model catalog today and see how my clients react," he said. "I'll let them know your limits. We might get some interest at some point, but I can't promise you anything. Most want models who are...open. I cannot state the importance of that. It all depends on my clients and your willingness to do what they expect of you."

"So until then, there'll be no work contract for me?" I couldn't hide the disappointment in my voice. No contracts equaled no job offers, which, in turn, equaled no money. "At some point" could mean anything. It could be the next week or next month. It could even be the next year. I had no time for waiting. Besides, patience had never been my thing.

"On the contrary, Jenna." He stood up, all six-foot-something of him, and his blue eyes penetrated me with amusement. My skin tingled with anticipation. "Five weeks."

"Five weeks what?" I asked, confused.

"Five weeks is all I can give you. After that, we'll see what happens."

In the distance, I could hear a clock ticking, reminding me that time was running out. I had to make a decision.

"I won't disappoint you," I said at last.

"Good."

Grayson returned to his seat and folded his arms. "Send Thalia back in on your way out."

I nodded, realizing this was my clue to leave. For some reason, I could sense that Grayson was irritated. I didn't know whether it was because I wasn't excited to do nude jobs or because he wasn't pleased with my answers. For all I knew, the interview had taken more time than he had intended to give it. Whatever the case, I decided not to analyze the situation too much.

I sat up and straightened my dress. "Thank you for taking a chance on me. It means a lot to me." I smiled and headed for the door, not waiting for his reply. From the corner of my eyes, I caught Grayson looking at my profile, his fingers rubbing his chin in thought. I wondered about his true impression of me, but even more so, I wondered what Jett would have said about my new job—if we were still together.

Chapter 5

"Woo-hoo," Thalia shouted the moment we were alone. "You're in."

As I stepped out of the building, the cold air whipped my hair into my face. I had no clue how late it was, but after Thalia's repeated, if not desperate, attempts to convince me to let her drive me home rather than take a taxi, I gave in. There was no sense in wasting money I didn't have or in hurting her feelings after she had done so much for me already.

Throughout the drive to Brooklyn Heights, I absent-mindedly listened to Thalia's recollection of all the jobs she had been booked for. I was physically present, but my mind was elsewhere.

It was clear to me that Jett's home was no longer mine and that I had to break off our relationship as soon as possible. Lots of people end relationships over the phone these days, don't they? To make sure he wouldn't reply, I figured I could call at four a.m. or during the day when he was at the office. I had no idea what I'd say, but I figured being short and blunt—without causing any more unnecessary drama—was the best way to go. Something like, "It's over. Don't contact me again. Bye and good luck screwing the next idiot. Oh, and by the way, I quit."

Scratch the last couple parts.

I had to make sure to let him know I was completely over him—without sounding spiteful or accusatory. To make sure, he didn't come back for answers, I would simply proclaim, "It's not you. It's me," in my most convincing tone, even though that wasn't entirely true. Of course it was always about them.

But what about the gifts?

Unintentionally, I touched the diamond pendant around my neck, realizing that it wasn't quite over until I returned the few gifts he had given me during our time together. Obviously, I couldn't keep them from a moral standpoint, as well as due to the fact that they'd always act as painful reminders of all the good times we had spent together. Happy times that had been nothing but illusions, cobwebs

46

of dreams and lies.

Leaving a phone message wasn't good enough. I'd have to write him a brief note and include it in a parcel I'd send together with the necklace. And maybe—sometime in the future, when I felt stronger and over him—I'd leave him a message on his answering machine to ask for my meager belongings, maybe tell him to *FedEx* them to me.

Eventually, we reached Brooklyn Heights, and I asked Thalia to drop me off around the corner and farther down the street from where I used to live.

Although I would have liked to consider Thalia as a new friend, there was no need to let her know my exact address. Trust wasn't easily built. While I liked her, I still had to build trust, not only to her but also to myself and to everyone around me. In the past few months, I had been more gullible than ever before. It had all been too easy to fall in love with Jett, to freely give my heart away, hoping for the best. I had been too quick to invite him into my bed and even quicker in my hopes to marry him.

Now I could see how stupid I had been and I wasn't ready yet—if ever—to return to my old life, to be the old, naïve Brooke who believed in fairy tales. If anything, the whole lesson taught me to never again trust a sexy guy in a tailored suit, and particularly not one with eyes as smoldering as fire, a body that could turn on the heat, and a voice that would melt away any woman's last inhibition.

As soon as we arrived, Thalia stopped the car. I said goodbye, then watched her drive away. For a few seconds, I stood under the street lamp, aware that I was alone on a deserted street in the middle of the night. I dreaded the imminent conversation with Sylvie almost as much I dreaded returning to an empty room in a tiny apartment, the meager surroundings I had lived in for many years before moving in with Jett. Deep down, I was afraid of returning to my old, lonely life.

My heart sank at the thought of that unknown future. Touching my stomach, I imagined my life without Jett. It was depressing to realize that I'd have to give birth alone to a child and raise her without a father. And how would I answer my baby's questions about her father was when I couldn't bear to ever see him again? Would I be able to cope? Work would keep me busy, but what would happen when I was alone—at home—in bed with nothing but my dark thoughts to keep me company? I could control those thoughts during the day, when I was busy, but I feared those moments of complete depression and utter humiliation at night, when my solitude would result in obsession and isolation, and all the questions and fears would come circling back. There was no doubt about the fact that, sooner or later, Jett would want to see me, if only to demand an explanation for my sudden disappearance and my avoidance of him—not because he cared, but because of his gigantic ego. I feared the moment when he'd appear in front of Sylvie's door. What if I wasn't strong enough to resist him? What if his words drew me back to him, because I was still not over him, and I allowed him to deceive me all over again?

I shuddered at the thought.

That can never happen, Stewart.

Never.

He had broken my heart in so many places I'd never be complete again. My heart still ached, and the image of them kissing would be forever etched in my mind. For the sake of my sanity, I had to stay away from him—if only I knew how.

Believing lies was easy when the truth was too painful to accept.

My hands itched to switch on my cell phone, because a part of me just didn't want to give up hope. I longed to hear Jett's voice, and yet another part of me wanted to make his life a living hell for destroying *us* and everything I had believed in.

The thought of taking him back after his betrayal enraged me so much that I quickened my pace, as if there was some slight possibility that I could outrun my own masochistic urges and stop hurting myself. Whatever his intentions, Jett was not good for me. Staying with him and allowing him to deceive me. Even seeing him again wouldn't be good for my mental health. It would all be too tempting to recount the positive times and forget about the bad ones; I'd foolishly forgive his cheating while allowing one excuse after another until my confidence would die like a frog in a boiling pot.

Somewhere in the distance, a bird screeched, and I couldn't help but think of Grayson's words about nightingales and the need to find one's path. For me, that path was just beginning.

Wrapping my coat tighter around me, I hurried to get to my destination.

The street was dark and eerily quiet. Police sirens echoed in the distance, and then the silence resumed. I rounded the corner. Ahead was the familiar five-story building. Other than a little light coming from a window on the second floor, all apartments were bathed in darkness. Reaching the front door, I tried to push the key into the lock when it slipped out of my cold hand and dropped to the ground, the sound unnaturally loud in the quietness. I winced. For a second, I had the image of someone opening a window and telling me to shut up, but no one stirred. As I bent down to recover the keys, I heard a different sound. Soft, thudding steps carried over from my right, and for a brief moment I caught a flash of movement, from the periphery of my vision.

Someone was following me.

My heart almost stopped in my chest, then picked up

with incredible speed. The hairs on my arms rose. I turned my head, panic rising inside me, and peered around me. I had been so absorbed in my thoughts about the future that it hadn't occurred to me that someone might be following or watching me. Not once had I bothered to look behind me.

Talk about being careless.

It was New York City—not exactly the safest place in the world at night. Pressing my handbag against my chest, I scanned the dark street again, ready to scream my lungs out of my chest if need be, but there was no one. The realization that I was overreacting didn't manage to calm me.

With shaky hands, I quickly snatched the key off the ground and let myself into the building, then slammed the door behind me. My breath came shallow and fast as I strained to listen for any sounds. Except for the wind swirling and hissing outside the windows, there was silence, but I couldn't shake off the feeling that, in that very instant, I was being watched.

Could it be Jett?

It had to be him. The thought that it might be someone else perturbed me. However, I had to take that into account and be prepared for anything. For a few minutes I just stood there, the image from before replaying in my mind on a constant loop while my eyes continued to scan the street outside the glass door.

Whatever that flash of movement had been, it had happened too quickly, and the thudding sound had been too sudden. Was it possible that I was being paranoid?

Again and again, my eyes scanned the streets. Apart from a few passing vehicles, the night remained as quiet as a tomb. No one walked past. No one emerged from behind the bushes and trees that were bathed in darkness. Eventually, I decided that maybe my nerves were overworked and my unsettled mind had played a trick on me. Not only was I tired, but I also had a hard day behind me.

Riding the elevator up to the fifth floor to our small apartment, I decided that I had to deal with my stress level. Jett had occupied my mind for too long; he had become a distraction from more important issues. If I wanted to build my life without him, I needed to take a break from even thinking about him. My thoughts and feelings for him had become a bitter poison to my soul, and there was only one solution: I had to get rid of them—the anger, the denial, the pity. Anything would do, as long as my thoughts stopped circling back to him and I would stop seeing his face in my mind. I figured, once I arrived home, I'd write a list so that I'd never forget what Jett had done to me and learn to accept what had happened in order to leave the past behind.

Chapter 6

I pushed the key into the lock and let myself in, welcoming the faint smell of my former home and the silence that seemed to penetrate every wall. Sylvie's designer handbag, coat, and heels were gone, meaning she was out, probably working late or on a date. Dropping my handbag on the old coffee table in the hall, I kicked off my shoes, and headed into the kitchen to make myself a sandwich. I ate slowly, taking measured bites, then slumped onto the bed in my room. My body felt exhausted, but I was unable to close my eyes and rest because of the racing thoughts in my mind.

Eventually, I couldn't bear the mental torture anymore. I

had to check if the legal firm had called back, so I switched on my cell phone, ignoring the hammering in my chest at the thought that Jett might have tried to contact me. I was afraid of his next lie, afraid that hearing his voice or even reading his texts might catapult me back onto dangerous terrain, where each word was like a double-sided blade: beautiful to look at but too dangerous to come close to.

The screen came to life and sure enough, text messages and call notifications began to pop up one after another. My skin prickled as my fingers swiped over the message button.

Crap.

Two text messages and eight calls. And all were from Jett.

Still no reply from the legal firm. But it was a weekend, so I wasn't particularly surprised. Sinking back against the cushions, I stared at Jett's name, a part of me wondering what he had to say while a different part of me wished I could just tell him to go to hell. While it wasn't like me to seek confrontation, the silence suffocated me. With a sigh, I unclasped the necklace from around my neck and locked it inside a drawer—the action making me feel better already, as though I was finally taking my fate into my own hands. Yet sadness continued to linger inside my heart. As the seconds turned to minutes, my indecision tugged at me, until I couldn't bear it any longer. I had to read his messages. At least one. Without hesitation, almost automatically, I opened the first text message.

Baby, I'm done at work and will be back at the hotel in 10 min. Can't wait to see you.

He sounded so innocent, it was ridiculous. Be back at the hotel? He had been there all along. What a liar!

Staring at the screen, I checked the timestamp, my hands gripping the phone so hard I feared it would break. The message had been sent half an hour after Thalia had picked me up, which meant Jett had probably spent the entire day with Tiffany—plenty of time for them to have a little fun in their private hotel room, probably laughing at my stupidity.

I smiled bitterly as I scanned the next message, sent an hour after the first.

Have you forgotten our date? WHERE are you? Let me know so I can pick you up.

My pulse raced at the obvious annoyance seeping from between the lines. Who the hell did he think he was? Did he really believe I would wait for him in a room all day while he enjoyed himself with someone else? Slowly, all the conflicting emotions that had been building up throughout the day erupted at once. The cold breeze turned into a raging storm. Not only was he a cheater and a liar; he was also trying to make *me* feel bad about not obeying his commands. The thought that he sought control over me made me so angry, I grabbed my pillow and threw it against the wall.

Forgotten our date? As if. For once, I wished that had been the case. Before I realized what I was doing, my fingers quickly typed up a reply message.

I want you to fuck off and get out of my life. I trusted your word, and you betrayed me. Don't deny it. I saw you with her. How could you hurt me like that?

My fingers lingered over the send button, hesitating. It would be the only message Jett would receive before I blocked his number forever. What was holding me back from sending it? In the end, I realized as much as I wanted to, I couldn't do it. I wasn't yet ready to admit to him the extent of my hurt feelings. Besides, what would be the point of letting him known how hurt I was? Or telling him I saw him with her? He'd only deny it and then he'd probably start calling, attempting to sway me over, and that I couldn't afford. Or, worst-case scenario, Jett would shrug it all off with no care that he had hurt me, telling me it was his right to kiss whoever he wanted.

My stomach did a flip. That would really be the tip of

the iceberg. We weren't married; I had no claim on him. But even though I could admit that to myself, I knew I wouldn't be able to hear those words coming from his mouth. Ultimately, I pressed delete in the hope that my refusal to talk to him and listen to any more lies would grant me the energy to stay strong and move on. I figured, as long as I didn't hear his voice or see him in person, the list of arguments I had put together would help me stay out of his path. And maybe, in time, my feelings for him would fade away. Come to think of it, now would be a good time to have Sylvie close by. But until she got back—

A soft knock jerked me out of my thoughts. I strained to listen, unsure whether it had been my imagination, when the key turned in the lock. A well of release rose inside me.

Sylvie was back.

It was about time.

I couldn't wait to pour out my heart and soul, and bitch about Jett. If anyone could help me—if only by listening and being overly annoying—it was Sylvie. She was the only one who knew how to distract me.

The doorknob jiggled before there was another frustrated *thud*, followed by a knock.

"I'm coming!" I shouted, figuring the door was stuck again. It happened often, particularly when Sylvie was so drunk that it took her a while to turn the key at just the right angle. Not her fault though. We had an old lock; the kind that had to be jiggled a few times. Sometimes, when it was really stuck, we had to kick the door hard, until the bolt released. We had been meaning to get it fixed for ages, but money was always tight and Sylvie too busy with more pressing issues than calling a locksmith.

As I hurried down the hall, I already felt better in the knowledge that I'd soon be able to share my misery with someone who cared.

"Just leave it. I got it," I said and pulled the door open.

No one there.

My breath caught in my throat, and my smile froze in place. As my glance swept over the empty hall, a sense of dread traveled down my spine. There were only two other doors in the corridor, and both were closed, but I knew someone had been there, because I was sure I had heard a key turning in the lock. The fact that the lights were switched on was proof that I hadn't just imagined it.

"Sylvie?" I asked quietly as I stepped into the narrow hall. Had she forgotten something in her car and headed back downstairs to get it?

Frowning, I bent over the railing and scanned the illuminated levels below, but there was no sign of her.

No sign of anyone.

"Sylvie?" I whispered again, unable to stop the trembling in my voice even though I *knew* it had to be her.

Why wouldn't she reply when I called her name? My

mind began to make up logical explanations. Maybe she was entrenched in her thoughts. Maybe she was making out with her date that instant, completely filled with lust and oblivious to everything around her. Still, why would she head back downstairs and not bring him up to the apartment like she had done with previous dates?

What if…?

No. I pressed my hands against my chest in fear and scanned the staircase again, suddenly aware of the faint sound of footsteps, then breathing. My head snapped in that direction. Without a doubt, the sounds carried up from somewhere below, near the stairs on the first floor.

My heart pounded hard against my ribs as the scene from earlier that day flashed through my mind: the strange movement, accompanied by the unsettling feeling of being watched. What if someone had followed me inside the building? But how was that possible, unless they had a key? Maybe I was being paranoid or, worse yet, developing a severe case of schizophrenia that was making me imagine things.

It'd certainly make sense.

Really?

God. Self-denial was bliss.

Then I heard it again—breathing and more shuffling. Listening intently, I held my breath. There was no mistaking he fact that someone was there that very instant, in the corridor below, listening to me, maybe even watching me, knowing I was scared out of my mind. A voice inside my brain urged me to move, but my legs wouldn't budge from the spot as my eyes scanned frantically for any signs, waiting for the predator to show himself.

Suddenly, the lights switched off, and everything went dark. I remained rooted to the spot, a pang of panic shooting through my body, crippling me. I turned my head sharply toward the weak light coming from the kitchen of our apartment. My heart pounded harder as my mind began to conjure up images of someone creeping up the stairs, ready to kill me. What if it was Jett's crazy brother? Out of all the people who had ever meant to hurt me, he was the most obvious choice, given the circumstances.

Getting inside and locking up was the only coherent thought I could form. As fast as my legs could carry me, I sprinted back to our apartment and slammed the door. My legs were trembling with so much force that I had to lean against the wall to stop them from giving out on me. My breathing was labored and as loud as a whistling train, and my mind kept obsessing over the identity of the person outside.

Could it have been Jett?

It had to be. I wouldn't have been surprised. He had always been sort of dominant, never taking "no" for an answer. The last time I had failed to answer his calls or texts, he tracked me down. I settled on him as the most obvious explanation; any other possibility would scare me too much.

Taking another sip, I leaned back against the cushions and pressed the cold glass of water against my throbbing temple. My eyelids felt heavily and I let them fall, the disturbing images of Jett with another woman drifting at the back of my mind and cruelly dancing there as I fell asleep.

***

From the periphery of my mind, I heard the muffled sound of a key turning in a lock and a door jiggling. Confused and disoriented, my head snapped in the direction of the noise. One quick glance at the clock revealed that I had dozed off for twenty minutes. Twenty minutes since someone had knocked at the door. Was it possible that whoever had been outside had hung around that long?

I jumped out of the bed, straining to listen for any more noises over my unnaturally loud puffs of breath. Finally, feet shuffled somewhere, and my heart began to hammer hard against my chest.

A door opened slowly and closed.

Not just any door. The door to our apartment.

Fear grabbed a hold of me as the realization kicked in

that whoever had been inside the building might have entered the apartment. All it'd take was the knowledge to pick a lock.

Retrieving the baseball bat Sylvie had once given me as a joke, in case we were ever burgled, I hid behind the door, mentally preparing myself to do whatever it took to protect myself and my child. My steps were slow and measured as I inched forward and raised the bat high, at head level, ready to bash. Eventually, the door to my room opened slowly.

"Brooke? Are you here?" Sylvie's blonde head popped into my line of vision. Her eyes widened with shock when she caught a glimpse of me. "Oh, my God, Brooke." She pressed a manicured hand against her chest and took a step back, her eyes filled with surprise and fear. "You scared the living shit out of me. I saw the lights switched on in your room, and I thought someone broke in. I almost called the cops, but then I let myself in and saw your shoes and handbag. Why didn't you just—" She stopped abruptly. A deep frown crossed her features as she eyed my face and then the baseball bat in my hand. "Are you okay?"

No, I wasn't okay, but where would I even begin?

It was all too much to deal with. My frayed nerves caused my hands and knees to tremble. I dropped to the floor, back pressed against the wall. All the tension I thought was gone, returned in an instant and stronger than before. I didn't even know where to begin. After all the crying and the self-blaming, I felt like an empty shell of myself.

"Brooke?" She inched closer and gently took the baseball bat out of my hands before she sat down next to me. Without a word, she wrapped her arms around me in a tight hug.

For a while, we sat there in the stillness, her warmth and touch the only thing that felt real. It was only after my limbs stopped shaking that I told her everything: the bad, the worse, and the blackest moment in my life. Recounting my memories almost ripped a hole in my chest, and yet, while the pain was all consuming, I didn't cry—because all the tears I had for him were gone.

Chapter 7

By the time I finished talking, Sylvie had almost emptied an entire bottle. When I insisted that she pour me a glass—not to drink it but to stop her from polishing it off—she adamantly refused.

"You can't drink in your condition." She patted my hand gently, her eyes blazing with anger. In all my life, I had never seen her so upset, especially when it should have been me who was full of fury. Sylvie wasn't the crier in our friendship. That was all me. Or at least had been upon finding out that Jett was cheating on me. Now my tears were depleted, and anger and humiliation had taken their place.

"Why are *you* crying?" I asked stunned.

"I'm not." She wiped a hand over her eyes to get rid of the telltale moisture at the corners.

"You're lying."

"Really, I'm not. It's just…" A muffled sob escaped her chest.

"Please don't," I said with enough determination to get her attention, afraid that her breakdown might tug at my own emotions.

"It just hurts me so much to see you in pain."

I had no reply for that. "It's okay. I'm fine. I got a job, and it pays well," I said at last, changing the subject.

"It's not okay, Brooke." She looked up at me sternly. "Don't do that. Don't just brush it all under the rug and pretend it's not there." She pulled a tissue from a Kleenex box and began to crumple it. "How could he cheat on you? You're perfect, Brooke. What the fuck is he doing with her when you're carrying his child? He was supposed to propose and marry you, not fuck the next girl. That isn't just a low blow." She inhaled a sharp breath, her eyes shimmering with the fury of a scorned woman. "It's the lowest thing any man could do. This is so fucking upsetting I feel like hurting him."

I smiled, touched by her loyalty. Luckily for the both of us, Sylvie was all talk, but not exactly a believer in violence. It was just the wine speaking. I could hear the liquid courage in the slur of her voice.

"Shit happens, Sylvie. You know that." I stroked her back in a soothing manner, but was only rewarded with a few tears trickling down her face.

"But you don't deserve it."

"I know," I murmured. "No one ever does." Seeing her crying and caring so much about me, even when drunk, made me realize just how much I had missed her in the weeks since I moved out. I could almost feel the intensity of her pain—as though she was more hurt than me. My vision blurred, but I didn't want to cry. My head was already throbbing so hard I was afraid it might burst.

Another tear rolled down her cheek, and she sniffled.

"Stop," I whispered. As hard as I tried to keep my own tears at bay, I failed.

"I can't help it," Sylvie said. "I hate what he did to you. I hate that he lied. He could have at least had the balls to tell the truth." She took another sip from her glass.

"That's what bothers me the most, too." I grabbed the glass of wine and pushed it across the table before she could take another sip, and squeezed her hands, forcing her to look at me. "I'll be okay. My heart will heal…eventually. It always does. Don't worry about me."

"But how can I not? You're my best friend, my sister, the kindest person I know," Sylvie said. "I saw how much that guy meant to you. You told me he was your first love.

He didn't have to go and give it away like that."

I shrugged. "I'll get over him, Sylvie."

"It's all my fault."

"How is that all your fault?" I asked, frowning, unable to follow her train of thought.

She moistened her lips and shook her head with a crazy look in her eyes. "It was my job to keep him away from you." She squeezed my hand so tight it almost hurt. "Brooke, I promise that I'll kick his door in and cut off his fucking dick. I'll make sure he'll never, *ever* use it again."

She looked so dead serious, I laughed out loud.

"No, you won't."

"Oh, I *will,*" she said with a deadpan face. "And you know what else?"

I shook my head and regarded her, amused.

"I'll hook you up with a real guy. Someone sexy. Somebody who'll make him eat his heart out. Together we'll find you a new boyfriend, somebody much better than what's-his-name." She leaned forward. "You have to take charge, Brooke. You have to hurt him the way he's hurt you, a leg for a leg."

"You mean, an eye for an eye?" In spite of the gravity of the situation, I found myself smiling.

"Yeah, that's it. Chick for a guy. Kiss for good sex. Whatever. By the time you're done with him, he'll be begging to get you back. Just promise me one thing." Her voice dropped to a conspiratorial whisper. "Don't ever let him into your panties again."

I nodded, confident that I could keep that promise. "I won't. I won't even think about it."

I was sure *that* would never happen again. But what about my dreams, my hopes, my wishes? My heart sank. Jett had cheated on me, and it hurt like hell, but sure as heaven, our time together hadn't been bad. He had made me feel good—most of the time.

Okay, that was a lie.

He had *always* made me feel good, that is until he cheated on me. And he also made me feel safe like no other man had before. As much as I wanted to push him away, there was no guarantee that, sooner or later, my body wouldn't yearn for his. It would start subtly, in my dreams, but as time progressed, it would get worse, until I'd see a little of him in every man who crossed my path. My subconscious mind would crave that time when I felt happy, safe, and in love. I prayed that before my subconscious took control, I'd meet someone new— someone who would replace him and would never let me down. And I hoped that special someone would give me the ability to control my sappy heart so that when I fell in love, I wouldn't drown in feelings.

"Let's go out." Sylvie's voice brought me back to reality.

"Maybe some other time," I said. "Right now, all I want

is some rest." I smiled at her in the hope she'd understand. The day had left me exhausted, eager to find solitude in the confined space of my previous room.

"Sure, sweetie. Whatever you want," Sylvie said, "but you owe me a girls' night out."

My smile widened at the idea of it: eating takeout, watching television, and laughing like schoolgirls until we couldn't breathe. I hadn't had one of those nights in ages and realized just I much I had missed it.

"Sounds great." Following Sylvie's advice, I headed for my room and collapsed into bed, ignoring the cell phone beckoning me from the nightstand.

Chapter 8

The next morning, to my surprise, Thalia called to tell me I needed to drop by Grayson's studio. I stepped into the kitchen and prepared myself a cup of coffee. Rain splattered against the windows, mirroring the way I felt: battered and depressed. Deciding what to wear from Sylvie's closet and preparing my makeup took forever. It took just as long to assure Sylvie that I was good enough to work on Sunday. By the time I reached Grayson's place, my hair was a mess and my back slick with sweat, but I had never been more excited. It was my way to cope with my nervousness over Jett's call; Sylvie had told him in her most nonchalant voice that I was going to stay with her for a few days because she needed me, hence buying me time to think about what I really wanted to say to him.

Like the day before, Thalia helped me change and did my makeup and hair; apparently, I wasn't fit to see Grayson the way I looked, and then I finally got to see the real studio. One minute I was chatting to the other girls, and the next Grayson came in and demanded our full attention.

"Watch and learn," Grayson called out to me, jerking me out of my thoughts.

I did as he said, albeit with apprehension at the thought of becoming one of his models. I sat in a swivel chair, with a bottle of water in my hand, and observed in silence, my attention once again returning from Jett to the task at hand.

On the west side, huge birch branches and plastic trees were decorated with white garland and pomanders in front of a backdrop support and lots of lighting gear. Grayson snapped picture after picture while communicating short but clear instructions on how each model was to pose.

I decided it wasn't going to be such a bad job, though it wouldn't be easy. Thalia had made an understatement in saying I'd just have to stand around and look sexy. Grayson's instructions were as varied as I thought they would be, and he kept each girl busy and on her toes—in all possible positions—albeit not nearly as dirty as I had imagined.

A tall woman, who looked as though she could walk the

runway in underwear, sat down on a broad flower swing, her hands holding on the ropes, while she crossed one leg over the other—harboring a dreamy look in her eyes. It looked sensual but not cheap or dirty. There was something elegant and almost classy about the way Grayson took the pictures, but even more fascinating was the way the girls posed in their colorful polka-dot dresses. I couldn't help but wonder if the pictures would be as beautiful as the models looked that instant.

"Jenna, hop in there," Grayson shouted, beckoning me over as he ushered the tall model off the set.

I almost fell out of my seat. "Me?" I asked incredulously. My gaze moved to Thalia, who smiled encouragingly at me.

"Who else? You know anyone else in here by that name?" Grayson's voice dripped with impatience.

Figuring he might decide to change his mind if I didn't move my ass, I rushed over to the girl on the swing. Grayson nodded, satisfied, and began to take charge.

At first, I felt out of place, but it wasn't as bad as I imagined it would be. He snapped a few pictures of us, then turned the focus on me. Following Grayson's clear instructions, I sat under one of the plastic trees, with my legs stretched out in a sexy pose, holding a closed, old book as if in thought. Another model peeked from behind the tree, as if trying to get my attention.

I had barely taken the position and gotten comfortable when Grayson called out, "Good work, everyone." He set the camera aside and began to clap, which I assumed was a sign that we were done. His applause was rewarded with more clapping from the models.

"As you all know, tomorrow we'll be hosting a big event, and the studio will be turned into a gallery," Grayson said. "I need each and every one of you here on time, so you can get ready." Grayson's blue eyes turned to me. "You too, Jenna. Thalia will fill you in." He turned back toward the group. "Gina, Sarah, and Thalia, you will pose for our guests. The rest of you will entertain, serve cocktails, and generally be your usual gorgeous selves. Make sure you give it your best. Whoever books a job gets a bonus. The checks will be in the mail. Do you have any questions?"

My heart began to race. I couldn't believe that Grayson was already inviting me to a huge event. For a second, I felt like hugging him, grateful that he had thought of me when I really had given him no reason to. Maybe me posing had changed his mind that I was worth taking a chance on, or maybe he was short of one girl. Either way, I was grateful for any hours he was willing to give me. Serving cocktails and talking to new people didn't sound so bad, particularly since I'd also be paid for it.

One of the sixteen models, a woman with short, platinum-blonde hair, raised her hand to get his attention.

"Yes, Sarah?" Grayson said.

"Sorry, I can't be here tomorrow. I have acting lessons."

Grayson ran his fingers through his hair, wearing an exasperated expression on his face. "Sarah, I counted on you. You knew I've been planning this event for weeks, so there's no excuse for your absence."

"I know." She shrugged. "I'm really sorry, but tomorrow's impossible. I tried to cancel, but the class is mandatory. The fee's already been paid, and I have to attend." She shot him an apologetic smile, the kind that would melt anyone's heart.

Grayson's expression didn't soften, and for a moment, I held my breath, anticipating his disapproving reaction. With his brows drawn and his eyes shimmering dangerously, I almost expected him to start shouting and throwing a tantrum, but his mouth just tightened into a thin line. Slowly, he turned his back to her, and his blue gaze scanned the group. Finally, those baby blues focused on me.

I could almost sense his intentions, yet I didn't dare hope. Instead, I just held my breath and waited.

"Jenna," he said sharply, "you asked for a chance, and this is it. You'll fill in for Sarah, but it's half-nude. Are you in?"

My heart jumped in my throat. The sudden silence was oppressing. Under Grayson's scrutiny, I peered from his face to Sarah's hopeful expression, then back to him, and I found myself nodding. He was right; it was my chance. Whatever he wanted from me, I'd do it. I had to. Even though, to be honest, I had no idea what half-nude meant, but it sounded better than being completely nude

"Yes, count me in," I said, my voice alien to my ears.

"Good. Then it's sorted." Grayson's grim expression barely shifted as he pointed to me, Thalia, and a girl with bright red hair the color of chili peppers. "You three will be posing and presenting. Don't disappoint me. I'm counting on you."

He expected us to do a great job, meet prospective clients, and earn him some new contracts. Given my retail background, I figured I could pull that off, even half-dressed.

***

"That was awesome!" Thalia shouted the moment we were back in the dressing room. She high-fived me and for the first time in what seemed like forever, I actually felt happy—as hard to believe as that was.

Before meeting Thalia, the thought of posing or modeling had never occurred to me. Now I couldn't wait to do it again. Things had gone so well. Not only did I earn my first real working assignment, but Grayson was extremely confident that he'd be able to place the pictures with one of his clients—in fact so confident that he had agreed to pay each of us $1,000.

A thousand dollars, which would go a long way toward paying the rent for the month.

The prospect of making money and meeting potential new clients excited me, even though I didn't have a clue as to what the job really entailed, except to be charming and help Grayson generate more business. Surely, compared to the nightmarish scenarios I had encountered in the past, Grayson's offering seemed like the Holy Grail on the path to improvement. Thalia had already shown me the sexy outfits wrapped in plastic, stuffed inside a huge box: brand new clothes that we were allowed to keep after the event. While they weren't exactly my style, the fabric was long enough to cover my private parts, and I was grateful for that.

"We should celebrate," Thalia said, interlocking her arms with Gina's and mine. "Tomorrow's going to be so awesome." Even she sounded like Sylvie—untroubled and free of the emotional baggage that came with a hot guy who turned out to be a cheater.

"I'm not sure we should get drunk before the big day," Gina muttered, squeezing out of her pink polka-dot dress and changing into a shirt and black jeans that did nothing to hide her beauty. With her porcelain skin and her bright red hair that fit her scowl, she kind of reminded me of a heated version of Arielle, the little mermaid.

"You're a sourpuss, Gina." Thalia nudged her playfully, then turned to me. "She's such a buzz-kill. Jenna, what do you think? Are you up for finding a bar and having a couple drinks?"

I laughed with unease. Now was the time to reveal my pregnancy, but I couldn't tell them and risk Grayson finding out when I had barely started the job.

"Maybe another time," I said. "I'm kind of tired."

"You guys are all so boring." Thalia scrunched up her face. "Another time, then. I'll call you up on it and then I'll have to insist we'll hit not one, not two—" She lifted three fingers as she counted "—but three bars. And I get to choose where and how we celebrate. Deal? But today—" Her voice dropped to a conspiratorial whisper as the corners of her smile twitched. "Today, I will dare you for one drink at the La Rue Bar, just one."

Gina and I exchanged glances.

"You're so bad," Gina said, laughing. "One drink, and that's it."

"Atta girl." Thalia's sharp gaze focused on me, and for a moment I could almost feel it penetrating the barriers of my mind, as though she could see right through me.

Just one drink.

I wouldn't even have to take more than a sip, and no one would notice.

Gina shot me a "trust me" look.

I had never really been much of a drinker anyway, no more than a glass or two of wine, but the idea of spending the evening with new friends brightened my gloomy mood. Besides, my obstetrician had even recommended one glass of wine every now and then. "Okay," I found myself saying and lifted one finger, "but one drink only."

"Absolutely." Thalia laughed out loud as she locked her arms with ours again. "That's totally the plan. Come on, girls. First round's on me."

Chapter 9

It was supposed to be one drink—just one single drink to celebrate the fact that I had found a new job. What's a night out without colorful cocktails or a cold glass of martini with a green olive on a stick? Ever since becoming pregnant, I had felt I had been missing out on the fun: New York City's nightlife screaming of light pleasures and dark chaos, quick dates, and drawn-out dramas—all the excitement and disasters that came with going out and not knowing how a particular night would end. At that moment, I hoped it would end in meeting new people, making new friends, and maybe finding the beginnings of a new life—a new path without Jett. Maybe even a new guy, someone who would take my mind off the past and help me move on.

I had worked hard all my life, but finding a new date, a new lover, someone to replace my past love, was harder—particularly in a city like New York that was full of people who had no time for relationships. The only available men for dating were those who worked at night: single, successful, driven, and eager to win and get ahead. Those who loved to work hard but fucked harder. They reminded me of my old self—eager to build a career, never looking for love or a relationship. If I wanted to get Jett out of my head, all I had to do was explore New York at night and meet new people. And all that started with a drink, albeit the nonalcoholic kind, whether I wanted it or not.

As we entered La Rue, the buzz of people and music immediately made my mind spin in a good way; the laughter and excitement all around me were surprisingly captivating.

"Let's sit at the bar," Gina yelled in my ear, "so we don't have to walk too far for drinks."

The bar area was so crammed, I doubted we'd find one vacant stool, let alone three. "There's a table over there," I said, ready to push my way through. For once, all the shoving and invasion of my space didn't bother me.

Thalia motioned to get the barman's attention and flashed her stunning smile, which had him heading for us in an instant.

I jotted down, "Cranberry cocktails—absolutely no

alcohol for me," on a napkin and pushed it over the counter toward him, with some money tucked inside. He winked at me, then took Thalia's order.

A few minutes later, we were sipping our cocktails at a table, our heads bobbing to the music blaring from invisible speakers that forced our conversation into shouts. Before long, one cocktail turned into two and then three, and I had to act as though I was drunk—which was fun, but not as much fun as watching my new friends getting hammered.

"She's single," Thalia shouted to a group of guys before I could stop her.

"Shush." I held a finger to my mouth, smiling. "You're making me look desperate."

It was true, but given her intoxicated state, I couldn't blame her. A few cocktails into the night and both Thalia and Gina were drunk. I had no idea how many drinks they had ordered already, because I had lost count at some point.

Ever since Thalia had asked about my relationship status and I had revealed I was single, she was hell bent on changing that by attracting the attention of potential suitors.

"You're not looking for anyone?" Gina asked, surprised.

"Hell, no." I shook my head. "I'm enjoying my single life." Both Gina and Thalia cast me curious glances. I waved my hand dismissively. "Long story, but getting into a new relationship is the last thing on my mind right now."

"Ah. Bad romance gone worse." Gina laughed. "I could

sing that song myself." She leaned in conspiratorially, her breath smelling of the mint gum she kept chewing. "Who needs love anyway when all you need is someone to warm your bed for the night."

I stared at her, open-mouthed. "Just to be clear, I don't want a relationship," I said. "I'm not ready for one now."

"Everyone says that after being dumped."

"I wasn't dumped," I protested.

"Sure." Gina winked at me. "You know, there's no shame in admitting it."

"What Gina is trying to say is that we can help you to hook up with someone," Thalia cut in, surprising me once again in her similarity to Sylvie. If it weren't for her exotic looks, she could have been my roommate's twin.

"We'll be your wingmen," Gina said. "Or wing women."

"Is that even a word?" I shook my head; it was easier than arguing with them in their determined and inebriated state.

"We'll find you a hookup," Thalia said. "No relationships. Just a hot guy who'll make you forget your ex."

I cringed inwardly. Yeah, as if that would happen anytime soon.

"That's the plan." Gina pushed her red hair back over her shoulder and stood to scan the room with the eyes of someone who seemed to have done this before. Several heads turned toward us and for a moment I wished I could just shrink in my seat so no one would see me.

"Please don't tell me you're looking for prospective candidates." I grabbed her arm and pulled, gently urging her to sit back down, but she wouldn't budge.

"As a matter of fact, she is," Thalia said, laughing. "Now sit back and let the professional do her job. Clearly, you need someone to help you move on, and when it comes to getting revenge, Gina's the best."

"No." I shook my head again and took a gulp of my drink. "I'm not looking for revenge. More like a rescue plan really, something to keep me running back to him." The words tumbled out through my cranberry-tasting lips, and I realized my blunder too late.

Thalia's eyebrows knitted together in a frown. "Why would you want to run back *to* someone? You call them an ex for a reason."

I shrugged. *Why would I want that indeed?* "I don't know. The sex was pretty good—amazing really."

"Here's what I usually recommend." Gina finally sat down, turning her attention back to us and wearing a determined look on her face. "If a man hits five on the list, you sleep with him, if only to feel shitty afterward and replace your good memories with bad ones."

My lips twitched as I tried hard to suppress the laughter bubbling at the back of my throat. Either they were making

83

fun of me, or the alcohol was speaking and they wouldn't remember a word the following day. "And what list would that be?"

"Clean, sexy, good-looking." She started counting and paused. "That's it. Everything else is a bonus." I didn't want to point out that she barely got to three points; maybe two since the term "clean" was debatable.

"She's right," Thalia said, her speech slurring more by the second. "It's hard to find a man who's caring *and* sexy, attentive *and* handsome. And don't get me started on supportive."

"Take it from me," Gina continued, "most men ran if I so much as asked them to water my plants."

Thalia nudged her. "You forgot to add hardworking but not completely obsessed with his career to the point of forgetting that you exist."

"So you suggest settling for less?" I asked, amused.

"No." Gina drew out the word and exchanged glances with Thalia. "What we're saying is that if you want to move on, you first need to get laid. There's no way around that." She paused for effect. "I know the perfect singles bar, and it just so happens to be down the street. Let's pay the place a visit."

"I hope you're not talking about that male strippers club again." Thalia laughed. Gina shot her a dirty look, shutting her up.

Strippers? Oh, God.

It was exactly what I had tried to avoid—running around from one place to the next, because I couldn't possibly leave them to their fate. They were too drunk for that, and someone had to make sure they got home safely. As much as I hated the idea, I couldn't just abandon them.

"You said just one bar and one drink," I muttered.

"I've changed my mind." Gina grinned and finished her drink in one gulp. "We'll help you, under one condition."

For some reason, I had a bad feeling. All that talk about sleeping with a stranger made me feel uncomfortable. I narrowed my eyes at her. "Which is?"

"*We* make the decision."

"What decision?" I asked, confused.

Gina smiled mysteriously. "We choose your guy of the night for you." At my shocked expression she raised her hands to stop my protest. " Wait. Hear me out. You don't have to sleep with him. Just promise that you'll date him for a couple hours."

I looked from Gina to Thalia in confusion. Friends choosing a guy for you? It sounded like a bad idea. I only had to think of my friends' disaster dates to know that hookups would end in the walk of shame, with my head buried deep in the sand. However, I also wondered what would happen if, for once, I let someone else make such a decision on my behalf. I wasn't exactly known for my good judgment in choosing suitable males for a relationship. Before Jett, I had only dated the kind of guy who couldn't commit if his life depended on it. And Jett...

I blew out a breath. He hadn't been so different than the others, what with his whole misguided idea about not marrying until we were old and gray. He had been such a bad decision. The whole falling-in-love-with-him thing had been a disaster. What if they had more luck than I had? What if a one-night date, a getting to know a complete stranger without having to sleep with him, was the solution, a way to move on from Jett and banish my memories of him—of being with him?

"Jealousy is still the best way to get back at someone," Gina debated with Thalia.

"It's not about revenge. It's about regaining your self-respect by knowing you deserve better," Thalia answered.

I held up a hand to stop their chatter. "Okay. I'll do it." I grabbed my bag and coat, ready to banish my memories of Jett to the back of my mind, if I hung on to them at all.

They stared at me until Gina gave Thalia a short pat on the shoulder. "You heard her. Let's go."

They grabbed their coats and bags in haste, as though they feared I might change my mind.

"But no more drinks for me," I said.

"Do you remember your address?" Gina asked, grinning.

I frowned. "Yeah. Why?"

"That's all that matters. A yellow cab will take care of the rest." Her face creased up in laughter. "Besides, I'm next in line to pay, and one last drink won't change your life."

I could only hope so. If only my feelings would stop telling me that she was wrong.

Chapter 10

When Gina had mentioned the singles bar, she forgot to add the fact that she was really talking about an underground club that looked like some sort of seedy, illegal establishment. Bass beats were blasting from inside, so loud my head began to pound before we even walked in. The entire building was painted black, reminding me of a graveyard. The entire atmosphere screamed bizarre, and definitely not my style. I should have already realized from the large, red "HUSH HUSH" neon sign above the entrance door painted in black that it was not the kind of establishment I would ever enter. But instead of arguing and standing my ground at the door, I clamped my mouth shut, waiting to see what could possibly happen next.

It was only when a guy covered in tattoos exited, his eyes assessing my body hungrily as his tongue brushed his teeth in a gross gesture, that I desperately wanted to run away.

"Are you insane?" I hissed at Gina.

"What? Are you scared?" Gina rolled her eyes and pulled at my hand. "Don't be a pussy. I've been here countless times, and it's great. Just wait until you're inside."

"That's probably open to interpretation," I muttered under my breath.

"You wanted a new date. This is where you'll find him," Thalia added. "In your circumstances, you can't be too fussy. You want to stop running back to your ex, right?"

I wanted to point out that *they* had *insisted* on finding me a date and that it had been all their idea, but there was no point in arguing.

"What's the password?" one of the five bouncers asked. He was a big man with greased hair and the most menacing expression I had ever seen. I swallowed hard and looked at Gina, inwardly praying she wouldn't remember.

"You'll never see it coming, Lewis," Gina said, unfazed, playing with her butterfly necklace. "Tonight I'll hook up with a hairy guy with large feet and small hands, get his number, then call him next week to tell him he has to go in for STD tests."

"That's harsh." To my surprise, the bouncer chuckled and, with a wink at Gina, he let us in for free.

"What was that?" I asked, confused, as we descended the stairs into what looked like a basement. "Was that the password?"

"There is no a password." She looked at me and grimaced. "Lewis and I go way back. It's just an inside joke we've had going on forever."

I nodded knowingly, even though I had no idea what she was talking about.

Eventually, we reached a dark corridor and moved past black curtains into a crowded room with silver lights that sent a sharp pain through my eyes. I closed them for a moment, unable to suppress a shiver. Slowly, I opened my eyes again and let them adjust as I took in my surroundings.

"Oh, my god," I exclaimed in horror.

The whole place was dark and hot, with no windows and no visible exits. Like the outside, the walls were painted a gloomy black. It was so hot and stuffy that I figured whoever owned the club must have installed heaters in the corners, probably to entice thirst so their clientele would buy more drinks. The walls looked shabby, and the whole place was in desperate need of some interior design. The tables and chairs were scratched and probably would have benefited from some scrubbing. I didn't want to sit down, let alone touch anything.

"It's awesome, right?" Thalia gushed, pointing to the stripper poles in the corners, where anyone bold enough was allowed to show off their abilities—or lack thereof. Judging from their awkward moves, the dancers were far from being professionals. "Everyone here's single, which is why they encourage rubbing up against anyone you like to see if they like you back." As though that was a good thing, she grinned at me and raised her eyebrows meaningfully.

"No." I shook my head slowly, fighting hard to stifle the onset of hysteria at the back of my throat. "I meant...Oh, my god. How awful," I murmured, unable to peel my eyes off the people dancing and making out in what looked like a huge pool, their bodies and clothes covered in foam.

I had heard of foam parties and had seen them on television, but I had never realized they actually existed and that they could be so wild. The people were uninhibited and probably intoxicated—and many of them were almost naked.

Someone bumped into me.

"Sorry," I mumbled and moved aside, only to slam into someone else.

Small rivulets of sweat began to trickle down my spine, both from the lack of space and from the stuffy air. I tied my hair behind my back and started to fan my burning face with my hand.

"Hey, Gina. Get those drinks," Thalia said. As soon as

Gina was gone, she turned to me with a frown on her face. "You're not going to pass out, are you?"

"What?" I stared at her. "No, I'm fine."

"Please don't tell me you've changed your mind about trying to find someone. I still remember how you looked when I picked up from Central Park. You didn't seem to be in a good place. It wasn't hard to figure out that you had been crying your heart out over a guy."

The image of Jett with Tiffany flashed through my mind, leaving a sharp stab of pain in its wake. I cringed inwardly. "Was it that obvious?"

She shrugged, as though it didn't matter either way. "No, but I'm used to seeing girls in your state of mind. Plus, you told me you were trying to move on from an ex and all that crap, so I figured out the rest. This might not be the most obvious place to visit after a breakup, but it's a lot of fun getting to know someone new, as long as you know what you're looking for." Her gaze lingered on a nearby couple, their bodies intertwined in a slow dance.

"I suppose so," I muttered and looked up to see Gina snaking her way toward us, balancing three pink-colored, and sugar-rimmed drinks decorated with sparkly straws and little umbrellas.

"They have the best cocktails in town." She handed each of us a glass, keeping one for herself, then continued to gush about the place. I eyed my drink warily, my brain struggling to come up with a good excuse to order my own.

"Drink up," Gina said, waiting for me to take a sip. "You'll need it when we go hunting for a guy."

To drink or not to drink? The question was a no-brainer. If I refused, I'd have to come up with an excuse. While I liked Gina and Thalia, I still didn't trust them enough to reveal my pregnancy, and I certainly didn't want to feel like the oddball of the group, the third wheel. I wanted to have fun, like a real New Yorker. I didn't want life to grip and hold me; I wanted to grip life and make it mine.

I lifted the glass and admired the beautiful pink liquid and sparkling granules of grenadine sugar around the rim. I took a sip and winced when the strong, sweet flavor hit my taste buds. It was delicious, leaving a sweet and tangy grapefruit zest behind—so delicious that I simply had to take another sip.

I didn't know if it was the atmosphere or the drink, but within a few minutes, the blood in my veins began to rush, my body growing lighter, until I felt like I was floating in midair. Usually, a drink or two didn't make me giddy and certainly not drunk, but I felt different this time, alive and excited—as if every fiber of my being wanted to move, dance, and act crazy. Even though I was scared of heights in any form, I felt as though I could jump off a cliff and into cold water, which I attributed to the alcohol mingling with my pregnancy hormones in a strange way.

"What is this stuff?" I held my glass up to Gina while continuing to sway to the rhythm of the music. Adrenaline rushed through my veins, as if the music inspired my body to be harmonious. Surreal happiness at the thought that I was young and ready to take on the world surged through me, a kind of blissfulness I had never felt before.

"My own personalized pink puddle drink," Gina said proudly. "It's my favorite. You want another one?"

Definitely not, but she was gone before I had a chance to stop her. It didn't take her long to return with another round of glasses, insisting that she show us the rest of the club. While I was reluctant to take another sip, the heat was slowly getting to me. I was thirsty and covered in a layer of sweat. Without Gina's noticing, I put down my first, half-full glass and took another one from her outstretched hand.

As we crossed the open-plan space at a snail's pace and pushed through the crowd, I began to see why the place was so popular. Everywhere I looked, people were dancing, talking, and having the time of their lives, just like I was. They seemed so carefree, which made me realize that in just a few months, I would no longer be like them. Soon I'd be a mother—bound to responsibilities and facing yet more bills. It might very well be my first and last time at HUSH HUSH or any other club, for that matter, and the thought scared me.

"See that?" Gina pointed to a circular area with dozens

of black wicker chairs. I nodded and she yelled in my ear, "It's the speed-dating area for singles...or those pretending to be."

The area was secluded, in the far corner, away from the dancing rooms and the foam party. Each booth had two wicker chairs facing one another, closed off by a string curtain that I assumed could be drawn, allowing for more privacy. The entire dating space was bathed in a violet glow, and was even darker than the rest of the club. I craned my neck to get a better view. A table was set up between each set of chairs. It was the perfect place to get to know someone without leaving the club.

"It works like this: you chat with somebody, and if you like what you see, you close the curtains." Gina took a sip of her cocktail, her eyes shining unnaturally bright as her eyes scanned the dating area.

I expected her to want to move closer, if only so she could show me around, but strangely, she remained glued to the spot, staring ahead as though she was waiting for something to happen. I had no idea how she could see in the darkness. While I could see the shape and movement of figures all around us, my vision wasn't sharp enough to make out faces. Eventually, Gina whispered in Thalia's ear, and they both turned to me.

I frowned. "What?"

What now?

Almost sensing their intentions, my skin prickled at the thought of what was to come. Gina pulled me closer to her, her eyes shimmering with pride as she spoke. She pointed her glass toward the northwest side of the dating area. "That one will do."

I followed her line of vision through the crowd and shook my head.

"Eleven o'clock," she said impatiently, "the booth closest to the wall."

Scanning the people around us, I narrowed my eyes.

Apart from two booths, all those close to the wall were empty. In the first one, a couple was engaged in deep conversation, the woman playing with her hair and laughing at everything the man said. In the second booth, a man was sitting alone—the only person close to the wall. From that distance, I could only see his profile, but even that was a blurry mess. With the dim and colored lights dancing above our heads, my vision was so impaired that I wasn't even sure the person was male at all.

"You mean the guy next to the couple?" I asked, just to be sure.

When no reply came, I turned to Gina, then to Thalia, who gave me an approving look.

"This is your chance, Jenna. That's *him*, your guy of the night," Gina said with enough determination to make me flinch. "I just know it."

I regarded him again. He looked unnervingly still. Unlike everyone else around us, he was just sitting there, motionless, not once turning his head to skim his surroundings.

My heart started to pound.

I couldn't just go over and talk to him when he didn't look like he was there for company. As I stared at him, pondering what to do, a woman approached the booth and sat down, leaving the curtain undrawn.

For some reason, I felt happy and relieved that it didn't have to be me. I almost squealed in delight that he wasn't alone and I was off the hook after all. I bit my lip hard to stop myself from smiling.

So, maybe I wasn't ready to date again. While my heart was still hurting in places, my mind craving distraction, and my brain screaming for revenge, I lacked the courage to approach a total stranger and start a relationship all over again.

"Such a shame he's found a date," I said, not meaning a word of it. I took a step forward, ready to leave the dating area behind, when Thalia's hand on my elbow stopped me.

"Look again," she said, pleased.

I turned back to regard him, just in time to see the woman stomp off. As she passed us, I noticed that her face was a mask of anger. Obviously, whatever he had said hadn't pleased her.

Nor me.

Shit.

Now I was out of excuses.

"Oh, come on." I remained glued to the spot, unsure of what to do, when a hand shoved me forward.

"What are you waiting for? Go talk to him before someone else spies him," Gina hissed in my ear.

She made it sound as if he was the last man on Earth, as if women were ready to fight over him. I wanted to point out that he was a human being, not a fish or an object to grab and pin to the wall. The thought of him being the last fish made me giggle. My nerves were making me irrational again, or maybe it was a physical reaction to stress and anxiety or the alcohol talking and letting me imagine all kinds of things in my mind. Whatever it was, my giggle turned into hysterical laughter, and before I could stop myself, I had taken a few more nervous gulps of my drink.

"I don't even know what to say," I said. "I'm not really experienced in approaching guys."

Actually, I was putting it lightly. Talk about having zero experience.

Swallowing down the rest of my drink, I composed myself. This was such a bad idea. But so had been drinking Gina's cocktail because, while I knew I was standing, I could barely feel my feet. Whatever had been in that cute little glass had sent the room spinning and my pulse racing.

It didn't send a rush of adrenaline through me, but it sure made me feel happy.

Gina rolled her eyes. "Just say, 'Hi. You look great. Want to hook up with me?' It really doesn't matter what you say. If he digs you, he'll be all over you anyway. Time to be slutty, bitch."

There was no way I would say any such thing, even if I risked being single for the rest of my life.

Shaking her head, Thalia turned to me and put her arm around my shoulders. "Don't listen to her. Just be yourself, Jenna. If it works, that's great. If it doesn't, you've lost nothing, and he's probably not the right one anyway. Remember, it's just for a few hours. Give it a try. You never know."

I took a deep breath. "All right." I handed Thalia my empty glass and stumbled forward, uncertain of whether I could fool my friends by hiding behind one of the curtains and then pretending the whole thing had been a major flop. As I spun around to find a flight route, I spied them in the distance, watching me like hawks, their hands waving at me, gesturing me to move ahead.

I decided I'd talk to the guy, who was probably boring and full of himself anyway. And it'd probably be over in no time. I laughed. Okay, so how hard could it be?

Chapter 11

With my heart pounding in my chest and my throat parched, I neared the man. How could they be so sure he was the right one for me? Did Gina have night goggles, or what? I was barely able to see his face, let alone the rest of him. What if he was a creep? I wondered what he had said to the woman that had caused her to storm off in a huff. Even worse than what he might have said, he might have just stared off into empty space, as though he was crazy.

Or maybe he was a killer with disturbing things on his mind.

I laughed inwardly at the dark direction my thoughts were taking.

Of course, a killer would hardly lurk in a bar with lots of people, would he? Unless he was a predator who didn't mind crowds—the kind I had seen in horror movies with lots of special effects and a creepy atmosphere—just like the HUSH HUSH bare. Even though this was real life, I couldn't shake off the feeling that it didn't differ too much from the movies. The bar was engulfed in darkness, and so was he, fitting right in.

Even from a distance, I could feel Thalia's and Gina's stares burning a hole in my back, eager for me to get moving.

"This one?" I mouthed and pointed at the man in my last attempt to sway their mind.

Please say no. Please say no.

Pointing toward the booth, I gestured again. But it was too late. The hairs on the nape of my neck prickled as something shifted behind me.

"Has no one ever told you not to trust a friend's choice over your own?" The voice was dark and smooth—the kind of voice that could hypnotize and send one into a trance.

Oh, come on!

Did he hear me talking out loud? Had he been watching us? My brain already fighting to come up with a lame excuse, I spun around slowly. I lifted my eyes to meet his gaze, ready to apologize, but my heart lurched at the sight of him, and I stumbled a step backward.

Holy pearls!

He was tall, around six-two. So tall I had to push my head back to see all the way up. Peering up into the darkest eyes I had ever seen, I swallowed hard.

He had a wolf's eyes. The kind of eyes that could undress a woman with as little as a glance—the kind of eyes that would haunt you in your daydreams. His raven hair was still wet, as if he had just stepped out of the shower. The sleeves of his shirt were rolled up, revealing strong arms, which were crossed over his chest as he regarded me with a frown. Dressed in a black shirt and black pants that accentuated his broad shoulders and his narrow hips, he looked as magnificent as the night.

There was something dark and brooding about him, something dramatic, something I was drawn to. His forehead was creased with lines, and his mouth was soft but unsmiling. Without a doubt, he was attractive—not sexy so much as mysterious, maybe even untouchable and unattainable.

I instantly knew that he was the kind of man who would take a long time to figure out. The kind of man I'd probably date as a rebound, only for fun and to boost my confidence, without giving away my heart. He was someone who could see me through hard times and make me forget—if only for one night.

The possibility flashed in my brain.

If only I wasn't scared as hell…

"I'm sorry." As I glanced back to my friends, my eyes searching for them in the crowd, I realized they were gone.

Of course.

They had done their job, and now I was left with a complete stranger.

"Sit down." He pulled a curtain aside, his hand touching the small of my back, leaving me no choice but to enter the empty booth.

I knew I should get far away from him, but for some reason I couldn't. I sat down on one of the chairs, my pulse racing so fast I was sure he could hear it. Nervously, I scanned the small space. His jacket was thrown carelessly over the back of a third chair. Car keys rested on the table next to a glass of scotch. The string curtain shielded us from prying eyes, but it also made the entire experience strange, almost intimate. The booth was small and poorly lit, and for a moment, I was happy that there were no walls—just hundreds of tiny black strings surrounding us. In case I needed to get away, it would be easy enough to make a mad dash.

The stranger pushed his chair close to mine. With my heart pounding against my chest, I watched him quickly close the distance between us and sit down. Maybe it was the violet lights reflecting in his eyes, giving them a brilliant, cold blue hue, but the way he looked at me, his gaze seemed to penetrate every layer of my soul. For a few seconds, I felt something between us.

Something clicked. Hot and tangible.

Passion?

Gina's words came to mind.

This is your chance, Jenna. This is him: your guy of the night.

I realized she might have been right about that.

"Your name?" he asked. Even the way he asked me screamed dominance, as though he was entitled to all—not just my name but also my body and mind.

"Jenna," I said my sister's name without hesitation and stretched out my hand in what I thought was a confident manner, though truthfully, all my confidence had flown out the door the moment he had turned his gaze on me. He made nervous, even more so because he was hard and beautiful.

Beautiful to look at, hard to hold on to.

He was like a beautiful angel carved in stone—not a peaceful seraph but the punishing kind, one who wouldn't hesitate to draw his sword and go to war to fight anything or anyone that stood in his path. An angel to fear. And fear was what I felt.

"Check." His hand reached out, and the moment his fingers curled around mine, an electric tingle ran down my spine. His hands were strong, warm, and callused. The kind of hands I wanted to grab and hold me right there, in that space, where I was floating.

My pulse raced.

"Check?" I asked, unable to stop the amusement from creeping into my voice as I repeated his name. "Check, as in…paper money?"

"Yeah, but more like a bill of exchange." He nodded slowly and for the first time, he smiled, revealing two rows of perfect, white, gorgeous teeth—teeth I could imagine nibbling on my lips. "It's not about the money though. It's about getting what others owe you. Do you like owing, Jenna, or would you prefer to be owed?"

My heart skipped a beat at the way he looked at me, and his voice sent shivers up my skin.

He leaned forward, closer, until I almost choked on my breath.

"How about I give you something so you'll owe me?" he asked quietly.

His words spun in my mind as I struggled to make sense of them. He looked like a lone wolf: wild, powerful, ready to pounce and ravish my body in a hard way. He was what Sylvie liked to call a DBM: a dark, broody, moody guy— someone who couldn't be held on to.

As I regarded him through the hazy curtain before my eyes, I realized I was drawn to him, not because he was my type—he was every woman's type—but because I recognized my own misery when I looked into his dark eyes. Something about him was like balm to my tormented soul, and I felt as though I was darkness longing to be with my own kind. He was the kind of man who could quiet a heart through the calmness he excluded, but most importantly, he was like the elixir I needed to become myself again.

"What do you want me to give you?" I asked quietly.

He raised an eyebrow at me and moistened his lips. Round, full lips that were worth kissing, and yet they were not Jett's. I hated that fact, but I hated myself more for thinking it. I hated myself for wanting Jett when Check was sexy and available, when he could help me.

Wanting a man only to use him to get over a broken heart was pathetic and yet…

"Sex." Coming from him, the word sounded like a demand. My skin tingled from his straightforward approach.

"Sex?" I repeated and laughed, the sound echoing eerily in my ears.

He didn't reply. Instead, his fingers began to tap on the table in a slow rhythm. They were long, the nails manicured. I stared at them, fixated, captured by the tiny movement that seemed to cause a rumbling roll inside my brain.

"And what would I get in return?" I asked, my gaze still glued to his fingers, which seemed to shimmer in the violet light.

"More sex. Better sex."

"Right." I giggled nervously. "Sex for sex?"

"And satisfaction," he added, "pleasure." He let the word roll on this tongue. "Quick, hot, toe-curling pleasure that you will never, ever forget."

As if it was even possible, he leaned just a little bit closer, so close I could almost feel his energy and his breath on my lips. Waves of something strong seemed to pour from him and into me, as though he was invading my mind, filling it with his, until I could no longer form a coherent thought.

"Sex can mean a lot of things, Jenna." His voice was calm, more forceful than before, and there was a hard edge to it. Or maybe it was his eyes, all dark and deep, as if they had somehow captured the entire ocean in them. They were so beautiful I could hardly focus on anything else anymore. "It can be meaningless," he continued, his fingers brushing over my hand, "or it can be full of adventure—the kind you've never experienced before. Which one do you prefer? The one that comes with no strings attached?"

I almost jumped back in shock as his hands brushed my knee, his thumb trailing the delicate skin.

"Or the kind that makes you feel you're being owned?" A flash of a grin grazed his lips, and I couldn't help but think that he was a master of seduction and persuasion. Not in an obvious kind of way, but his technique seemed to work.

I groaned inwardly as the realization dawned on me. As I stared at him, I understood why the woman had run away. The guy wasn't a creep. Check wasn't there because he was single or looking for a date.

Come on. A handsome stranger called 'Check', asking for instant sex. What do you think he is, Stewart?

Holy dang. He was a male prostitute and anytime now he'd disclose his price per hour. It was so obvious I almost slapped my forehead for not realizing it sooner.

I stared at him, disgusted.

"How stupid do you think I am?" I asked, shame and humiliation burning through me. I gulped down a large mouthful of air before I continued, "I don't have the money, and even if I wanted to have sex, which I don't, and even if I wasn't a $100,000 in debt, I'd never sleep with a prostitute."

I grabbed my bag and stood on shaky legs, ready to storm through the curtains, just like the other woman had, when the room started to spin so fast that I fell. Somewhere to my right, a glass smashed against the floor. Strong arms grabbed me before I hit the floor. I flinched, fighting the urge to sink into them.

If only he wasn't—

"I'm not a prostitute," he hissed in my ear as he helped me up.

He wasn't?

I tried to stand and apologize for knocking over his glass, but my words remained trapped behind my lips. The alcohol rushing through my veins was strong enough to make my knees give way beneath me. Were it not for his hands holding me, I would have tumbled to the floor.

"I'm sorry." I felt silly for my outburst, for knocking over his glass, and for the nonsensical accusation; for my body being so drunk I was out of control.

As much as I wanted to explain, my words failed me. My mind was a blurry mess, my thoughts rushing around like the tumult at the bottom of a waterfall. Everything, from the stranger to the room, was spinning fast. I closed my eyes again, and before I could stop myself, I leaned my head against his chest, until the spinning slowed down and I felt better.

"Are you high, Jenna?" he asked from what seemed like a million miles away.

I shook my head. The thought that I was high was so absurd I laughed out loud. "I'm most certainly *not* high. Trust me, I would know if I was." I peeled myself off his chest and met his gaze.

For some reason, I expected him to smile, but he didn't. His face was a serious mask, his mouth was pressed into a thin line, and that frown was on his face again.

Clearly, he didn't believe me.

The thought that the handsome stranger thought I was a drug user when I had barely had a cocktail enraged me, and my temper flared.

"You know what? You have no right to judge me." I pushed a finger into his chest, marveling at how hard his body felt. "It's not your right to be accusatory when you don't know me. I've had a rough day. Maybe I look like I'm high and sound drunk, but you know what? You sound and look like my cheater ex." I pushed out my chin defiantly as I stared him down.

He looked taken aback.

Pushing his arm away, I tried to put some distance between us, but he held on to me tight, until I could almost sense the beating of his heart, calm and steady.

"A man who doesn't respect his woman isn't worth keeping," he whispered against my earlobe, his voice caressing every nerve ending. "No woman deserves to be cheated on. I'm glad you ditched the bastard."

"Yeah, so am I," I replied and wiped a hand over my eyes before the telltale moisture could give away my state of mind. His words, short and superficial as they were, touched me.

For a few moments, silence lingered between us, but in that moment I felt as though he understood me and the pain that seemed to creep up on me again.

"I'm sorry if I offended you," he said eventually.

"I'm sorry I insinuated that you are a sex worker," I replied and stifled a giggle.

Maybe it was the way he touched the small of my back—so tenderly, as if his hands knew how to make me feel good—but my anger faded instantly. Or it might have been the warmth of his body, but something about him seemed to calm down the storm brewing inside me.

I leaned my head against his chest, wondering what would happen if I let him in and took him up on his offer. Would my heart be free of pain—if only for one night? I pushed my dark thoughts to the back of my mind, where they could no longer reach me. On that night, I didn't want to be alone with my demons. I didn't want to think about the past. I wanted to be with a stranger, with someone who would make me feel good. Then, as soon as the night ended, he could just disappear from my life.

Gina was right. I needed something uncomplicated.

"I want to try it," I whispered.

"And what would that be?"

"You asked me what I want," I started, choosing my words carefully. "I want you to have a drink with me…at my place."

There was silence. Waiting for his answer, I held my breath.

"You know what you should never do?" he said eventually.

"What?"

"Hook up with a random guy and let him drive you home." His voice was still serious, but now he winked at me with a devilish grin.

I giggled. "That's the plan. If I have to sleep with a total stranger, I'd rather it be you."

"Why me?"

My skin tingled from the magnetic pull between us.

"Because—" I stopped, looking for the right words. Granted, I didn't know him, so what could I possibly answer? That I felt attracted to him because he was physically attractive? That I didn't want to be alone at home and face my inner demons? That the alcohol rushing through my veins had made me horny, and the prospect of sleeping with him was appealing?

"Because you want me?" He raised an eyebrow at me, leaving me both wanting and fearing him.

I nodded and whispered, "And more so because I need you."

And because there is no *us*. No chance of another heartbreak.

As though to test my boundaries, his hand brushed my ass while the other forced my chin up. Ever so slowly, his lips neared mine. For a second, I thought he'd kiss me. I held my breath, awaiting his hungry mouth. To my dismay, his lips traveled up my neck and brushed my earlobe.

"I'll take you home." His tone left no room for discussion. His grip on my arm tightened as he led me away from the booths and out door, toward his car.

I stopped in midstride and spun slowly to take in my surroundings. Maybe the darkness in the club had wreaked havoc on my vision, but everything shimmered bright and colorful, as if the entire night sky had captured auroras. It was so bright it hurt my eyes, and I had to close them for an instant.

Eventually, I got into the car. As we drove home in silence, I leaned my throbbing head against the cold window, listening to the soft rain splattering against the windshield, my mind strangely devoid of thoughts. Everything—from the car seat to his cologne—smelled expensive, suggesting that he was someone who knew what he wanted, someone who liked to take charge.

For the first time, I wondered if it was such a good idea to bring a dominant stranger into my home when I was already lost in the jungle that had become my life. I kept my eyes closed against the dreaded sleepiness threatening to creep over me. Before I fell asleep, the car stopped, and I peered into the hazy darkness.

"We're here," Check said.

I got out, waving him over. "Let's go inside."

Strangely elated, I exited the car and fished for the keys in my handbag. As I tried to push them into the lock, they fell to the floor.

"Let me get those for you," the guy whispered and picked them up. Before I knew it, he had let us in and we were in the elevator, his strong hands pressing me against him as he steadied me.

Alarm bells began to ring at the back of my mind, warning me of something I wasn't seeing. It was so obvious that I could almost grasp it, yet the knowledge seemed so far away. But instead of following that worrisome train of thought, I closed my eyes to escape the dim lights and let him follow me into my apartment.

Chapter 12

The soft light of the street lamps streamed through the large windows, casting a golden glow on the heavy furniture and the rug that covered most of the hardwood floor. We crossed the hall and entered my bedroom in haste, the stranger stifling my giggling and the loud drumming of my heart with his hand grabbing mine. The room was bathed in darkness, but I didn't switch on the lights. Why bother when I didn't want to remember the stranger's face, nor the events that would follow? No attachment, no recollection— nothing that would remind me, so the deeds were best done in the dark.

That night, I didn't want to be me. I wanted to be

someone who was free from pain, free from the past and hopeless dreams of a future that would never be mine.

I liked the idea of sleeping with him and, come dawn, he'd be out of my world. I liked the anonymity, the no-getting-to-know each other, the detachment of it all. It was like confiding in a random stranger, except that instead of sharing secrets I'd be sharing my body in the hopes that it would make me feel better and allow me to move on from my past and help me banish any memories of Jett—if only for a few hours.

"Do you want a drink?" I peeled myself from the stranger's embrace and turned to face him, my gaze hazy in the night. Ever since I had invited him to my place, he had remained quiet, and not just throughout the drive. Standing near the door, his intense gaze lingered on me as he watched me with an unreadable expression.

His confidence made me nervous, and I lowered my eyes to the floor in the knowledge that a man like him—too assertive, too commanding—who visited that kind of club must have had many one-night stands with countless women. I was certain that was where he'd gained all his obvious experience.

"Lie down," he said quietly but with enough force to make me follow his command.

Silence ensued again, and for a moment, I just stared at him, unsure of what to do.

"So, um…Is there anything specific you want from me?" I asked when the silence became uncomfortable and the entire situation began to feel surreal. The insecure edge in my tone was evident, but I didn't try to hide it. I had never had a one-night stand before—at least, not a real one—and I had no idea how they worked.

Already, everything felt bizarre. The room was slightly spinning, and I felt as though I was trapped in a dream. Maybe it was a dream, because in my blurred vision, everything—from my matchbox room to the man standing before me, motionless like a statue—seemed larger, unreal. His size intimidated me, and his stare frightened me, but not to the extent of making me want to run.

Finally, I heard his slow, muffled steps as he moved closer, stopping inches from the bed. "I have to go."

Even in my ears, his excuse—or lack thereof—sounded weak, dripping with hesitation and something else.

Anger?

Defeat?

You're misinterpreting too much.

"Why?" Frowning, I stared at him. In the darkness of the room, I couldn't read his expression.

"Because I won't take advantage of a drunken woman. That's why," he whispered. "The only reason I agreed to give you a ride home was to make sure you got home safely. I didn't want you to take a cab all by yourself or, worse, to end up going home with the wrong guy, someone without my...integrity. You never know what might happen if you go home with a stranger. Some other guy might use your inebriated state to take advantage of you."

A man of morals. Great.

Even though his concern touched me, I laughed bitterly. The fact that he wanted to leave so soon filled me with despair and rejection. Back at the club, he had been so sure of our interlude, shamelessly flirting with me. Now, doubt had replaced the need I had sensed in his tone.

"I'm not drunk," I said, certain that I couldn't be. I hadn't even finished two cocktails.

"Get some rest. You don't look too good," he whispered.

I was feeling a little sick, but not so much that I wanted him to leave. I couldn't bear to be alone with my dark thoughts. My demons were too forceful, struggling to be let out.

"Please, don't go," I begged. Swaying slightly, I grabbed his hand and pulled him to me. He sat down the edge of the bed, keeping a few inches between us.

I didn't know what else to say. How do you stop a stranger from leaving you alone in a pit of darkness? The desperation in my voice spoke more than a thousand words. Never before in my life had I been so nervous and desperate at the same time. The body I was in didn't even feel like me. It wasn't *that* crazy to sleep with a stranger. It wasn't *that* desperate, or so I kept telling myself. He had to pick up on it because if he didn't, I wouldn't be able to stop him from leaving.

I moistened my parched lips. "You said you like when people owe you," I began and, suddenly remembering his name, I added, "There is something you can do for me, Check. I'd like to owe you."

"You already do. I brought you home," he said.

I shook my head slowly and frowned as the haziness intensified. "No, that's not what I meant."

"What else do you need from me?" His fingers lingered over my hand, as though he couldn't decide whether or not he should touch me.

"I want you inside of me." My voice came raspy, alien to my ears. Had I always sounded so vulnerable? Come to think of it, it wasn't crazy to sleep with a stranger. It was despair. If that would keep him for the night, then so be it.

Pushing my legs on either side, I moved onto his lap. If I played my cards well enough, maybe he would give in. So, I leaned into him and trailed my fingertips down his shirt. Under the fabric, I could feel rows and rows of hard muscles.

"Is that a suggestion or a demand?" he asked huskily, giving up control. I liked the idea because it gave me power when I had lost control over my real life.

"Both." My voice sounded hoarse, matching the low rumble in his throat. Satisfied with his reaction, my hands interlocked behind his neck. As I bent forward, I smelled the faint scent of scotch and something else, and my heart began to pound in my chest. Slowly, I brushed my lips against his and sucked on his lower bottom lip as I moved my hips against his growing erection, back and forth, until his breathing grew heavy and his length hardened, straining against his pants. Below me, he was becoming as hard as a stone. I only realized he pulled back when his arms wrapped around my waist. At first, I thought it was to initiate sex, until his grip tightened, stopping my movements.

I frowned.

"What's wrong?" I asked, confused. He wanted me, no doubt about that.

"Your offer is tempting, but—" He paused to consider his words.

"But what?"

"You're wasted, and as I said, I'm not comfortable taking advantage of you or your body."

I laughed. He just wouldn't let it go.

"Does it really matter? You're here. I invited you, and I'm obviously consenting." I sounded pissed, but I couldn't help it. "Or am I not sexy enough for you to fuck me?"

"You're sexy enough and then some. There's no doubt

about that," he whispered. "But I can't control myself. If we continue, I'll feel as though I violated you in the most intimate way, and that doesn't work for me. I don't want to lose control and hurt you. That's not my intention."

"I don't believe you," I said, shaking my head. "I should have known you don't really find me attractive. There's no reason for you to lie. You could have told me you're not interested before you dropped me off. I would have understood." My tone betrayed my disappointment and hurt, but I didn't care. He was rejecting me and had wasted my time, not to mention humiliated me. Tears began to roll down my cheeks. I wiped at them angrily as I stood, feeling strangely emotional. "You can go now."

His footsteps thudded behind me. The door was just a few steps ahead. I reached it and opened it, planning to slam the door after him as soon as he walked out.

I wanted him to leave—better now than later, when things became awkward and I began to analyze what was wrong with me.

I was hardly out of the room when his hand clasped around my upper arm and he pressed me against the wall. I fought against his iron grip, but he was stronger. Faster. His lips descended on mine with a hunger that wasn't natural. For an instant, dread filled me, but strangely, his roughness turned me on.

"You want me inside?" he asked hoarsely. His dark

voice sent a throbbing sensation between my legs. Together with his scent and the intensity of his touch, it was a heady combination.

I was lost, bent to his will.

Dipping his tongue into my mouth, he gripped my wrists and pulled them above my head. I moaned as our tongues met in a dangerously slow dance—circling, teasing, and testing boundaries. His hands began to move lower, past my abdomen, and cupped my ass until something hard brushed me.

"Where do you want me to fuck you?" His hoarse tone dripped with sexiness that made my stomach quiver.

I knew he was testing me to see if I would express second thoughts, change my mind, maybe even push him away. Even though I knew I couldn't let his male dominance win me over so easily, my body ached for his touch. So I did what I had to do: I pushed him away and slowly pulled down the zipper of my dress. With his eyes on me, I let my clothing drop to the floor, until I was standing in front of him with nothing but my panties on. I looked up and smiled, knowing he had no choice but to honor the end of our unspoken agreement.

"Wherever you want," I said at last.

"You're giving me a choice?"

"For once, I don't want to be in control," I whispered and pulled him close to me.

Our lips connected, this time with more fervor. My mouth opened to allow him deep access. His hand moved between my legs to touch me with hard, determined moves. For a moment, my breath caught in my throat at the realization that a stranger was touching me, and I welcomed it. I would be lying if I said that I enjoyed it, but it was what my body needed. Quivering, I leaned against the wall, clawing at his shoulders, demanding that he fill the void inside me.

"Remember, this is what you wanted. Once I start, you can't change your mind. Is that clear?" Check asked and I nodded. "You better not complain."

I shook my head. "I won't."

His kiss grew more demanding, his hands impatient as he lifted my ass and raised me onto the large sideboard. In one swift movement, his fingers pulled down my panties, then spread my legs before he slid between them.

My head throbbed hard; my legs began to shake, and my heart raced in my chest—but not from his probing fingers or the hot sensations they sent through me. Maybe the cocktail Gina had bought for me had been too much in my pregnant state, but his presence intermingled with the alcohol, and the whole new body experience of not controlling myself, together with the prospect of having sex with a stranger was overwhelming, if not a hell of confusing. I felt like I was dropping from a skyscraper and floating in midair. His kiss, his touch, his hardness felt like molten lava pouring through my body. I felt like I was outside of time and space where nothing made sense, where I was walking through muddy waters, and at any moment, I would sink into a black hole of a dream if I didn't hold on to this stranger. My core had to be raptured soon, or else I feared I would no longer be able to decide what was real and what was not.

"I like hard floors," he whispered. With one hand, he pushed me down until I was lying flat on the smooth wood, my naked body exposed. "The only reason we're not in your bed is because I'm going to fuck you right here against the sideboard, then on the floor." As though to prove his point, his fingers began to rub between my folds.

"Oh, my God," I whispered when his tongue swiveled around my navel, then trailed down my abdomen and settled between my legs with a precision that hardened my nipples and sent my fingers balling into fists. He was so good, and yet I couldn't relax.

"You want me inside you?" he asked, but he didn't wait for my answer. "Not yet. This is what you're going to get first."

He groaned and dived a long finger into me, followed by another, while his tongue circled my bud, kissing and sucking in equal measure. I arched my back to meet his knowledgeable mouth and suppressed a moan. He could have all he wanted. He could do with me whatever he wanted. Nothing would break my resolve to sleep with a stranger.

Somewhere inside my brain, a voice urged me to stop, warning me that I was only hurting myself, but for once, I didn't care. What could be worse than the pain I was already feeling? I wanted to be ruptured, to be penetrated, to be handled roughly—anything to divert my mind from my broken heart. The stranger fulfilled the desire just fine.

Slowly, he pulled out his fingers. I opened my eyes in surprise when a soft breeze hit my sex, and I prepared to protest when his hard gaze stopped me.

"You're not wet enough, and there isn't enough space for us both in this room. The floor will have to do," he said, as if that explained everything.

In another swift motion, he swooped me up in his arms, only to lower me down on the hard floor. Lying on my back with my legs spread apart, I felt like his prey, and for a second, I thought he was like a wolf, eager to devour me. The moonlight streamed through the windows, barely illuminating our features. As I stared at him in the semidarkness, I saw his eyes glinting. His lips curled into a forceful smile, and in that moment, he really looked like the wolf I had compared him to. His eyes were squinted, and his teeth sharp. His skin was unnaturally pale. Judging from the way he was leaning over me, he looked like a big creature that was about to kill me.

Come on, Stewart. A wolf? Seriously?

I frowned.

But how? Was this a dream? Was I so drunk that I couldn't discern reality from fantasy? Peering up at the ceiling, I could see small spots, like stars, and they looked like they were falling, more proof that I was trapped in a dream. The thought pleased me.

Yes, I could deal with it all being just a dream.

A dream was the only explanation for the picture in front of me. I had to be still asleep in his car, or maybe the day hadn't really happened at all. My gut feeling told me there was more to the fantasy than I was grasping. Sure enough, he shifted from wolf to human being again. Focusing on him was impossible though. The room remained as dark as a big, black hole, spinning, twisting, and turning like a hypnosis picture. Even the stranger looked skewed.

Somewhere, I heard the sound of foil tearing, but I didn't lift my gaze to look at him. Deep down, I knew I was still afraid of what was to come and that I'd change my mind. I was afraid of his penetrating gaze and of letting myself fall into whatever he had to offer.

The realization that I wasn't ready flickered at the back of my mind. I took a sharp breath and let it out slowly. It was too late to change my mind, not after I had asked him to join me. In my mind, all I could see was Jett—the way he had smiled at me, the way he had touched me.

Damn it!

I smiled bitterly. That sneaky bastard was already creeping back into my head, consuming me, and my foolish heart just wouldn't stop loving him. In a distant memory I could still feel the pain of his betrayal, the betrayal of my heart, and a hint of remorse, all intermingled with the knowledge that revenge would never repair the damage he had caused. Because of him, I was sleeping with a stranger. But I had to do it even if it was just a dream.

Banish it. Forget him. Don't linger.

It was too much. Too painful.

I had to prove to myself that I was strong enough to move on from him, or else I would always compare every man to him, and no one would ever be good enough for me. I had to stop feeling and seeing Jett in every breath I took and in every stranger's face.

It was no longer about love. It was about releasing the physical pain inside me. It was about freeing myself from my addiction so I could feel alive again.

"You're pretty," he whispered, his hand touching my face. I didn't look up at the stranger, not even when he spread my legs and lifted them until they were almost up to my chin. As he lay down, his hard erection brushed my entry, and his hand rested inches from my face. I shuddered and turned away. The knowledge that he was about to enter me chocked me to silence, and yet I still didn't see it coming.

As he dived in, I gasped.

Holy crap!

He was big and hard. My muscles instantly cramped around his thick, pulsing length, eager to both let him in and push him away.

"Oh God." I winced and squirmed as I tried to wriggle out from under him, but his hand stopped me.

"Don't." It was just a word, but there was something sexy about his tone.

I fidgeted to accommodate his size, and then forced out the breath I had been holding. Slowly, he eased into me, filling me, stretching me, burying himself until I could feel him pulsating deep within my core. I whimpered in protest when he pulled back, only to dive in again, repeating the friction while sending equal jolts of pleasure and pain through me.

"Does it hurt?" His voice was strained with desire and concern.

"Not anymore," I lied.

"Good." He wrapped my legs around his hips and eased into me carefully, as if he was afraid he might break me. I doubted he could do more damage when everything was already broken.

His movements of withdrawing and thrusting, each time going a little deeper, sent a jolt of heat through me. Something began to pulsate, strong and hard. I lifted up on my elbows, my mouth finding his in the darkness.

Somewhere in the back of my mind, the thought registered that my body belonged to another man, but I didn't pursue it. I didn't think about the implications or the fact that, in spite of my physical lust for him, every fiber of my heart screamed in protest, because the stranger wasn't the man I wanted—not for the night and not even in that dream. He was simply someone who filled the emptiness within me.

Without my permission, a tear trickled down my cheek. Even though it was dark enough, I turned my head away so he wouldn't glimpse it. At least Check wasn't a psycho, and he had been kind enough to ask if I was okay. How often do you find that kind of attitude? He wasn't that bad.

"I want to reach every inch of you," Check whispered as he plunged into my sheath, hard and fast, again and again until my skin was entrenched in sweat. My body began to tremble from lust—not because of him, but from the image that kept flashing before my eyes: Jett's face, his sinfully green eyes, his full lips, his sexy, tan body. They were past memories of Jett, but even in that moment, with another man inside me, my mind wouldn't stop wishing it was him taking me, spreading the moisture deep inside me. Come to think of it, the way Check touched me, the way he moved, the way he moaned, even the way he was holding and kissing me reminded me too much of Jett. I wanted to scream with frustration.

Just sick. Even now, you keep thinking about Jett.

What was wrong with me? Why was I so turned on by the images in my head?

It was too much to bear. I pressed my eyes tightly shut until white spots appeared in my vision.

"Fuck me harder," I demanded.

Do anything that will dissolve this image; take me away from this craziness.

"As you wish."

Pinning my wrists above my head, he thrust in and out, stretching me, entering me deeper and faster, until the tiny movements became as hot as fire. He was so raw, so primitive, that I could feel my insides quivering in both fear and delight. He cupped my ass and lifted my hips, inviting me to meet his thrusts, and I did so willingly, surrendering to the wildfire spreading inside me and the new sensations washing through me.

At least, I felt like I was still alive.

The way he filled me and circled his hips was intense and powerful. Lifting my legs higher, he entered a new level of depth, all while the image of Jett continued to haunt me, turning me on. As Check slammed into my willing body one more time, a moan fled my mouth, and I could feel myself tightening around his erection. A cry escaped my lips seconds before I came, falling apart around him.

"Fuck, Brooke." He groaned seconds before he found his own climax, releasing my wrists and letting me go as he moved aside, freeing me from his weight.

My heart skipped a beat.

Brooke?

Wait. How did he know?

I froze.

What a stupid, crappy dream! What a load of shit! But what if it wasn't just a dream at all?

My brain struggled to fit the pieces of the puzzle, and as it did, I realized something more awful, something that hadn't crossed my blurry mind until then. How did he know where I lived? I had mentioned Brooklyn—that much I remembered—but I never told him the exact address. I was sure of that. So how did he know where my apartment was situated? How did he know my real name?

My heart spluttered in my chest. I opened my eyes, clutching at the floor for support. But before I could ask any of the questions burning inside my mind, the sickening spinning started again, amplified by the blood rushing from my orgasm. As I rose to my knees, everything faded to black, and I could feel myself falling, welcoming the darkness with a last fleeting thought: Who was the blue-eyed stranger I had brought home?

Chapter 13

The next morning, I awoke to a throbbing sensation inside my head. The soft light of the early-morning sun illuminated the bedroom, sending jolts of pain through my body. Everything was hurting: my legs, my head, even my eyes, which felt heavy, as if they were glued together. Blinded by the glaring brightness, I closed my lids again. In spite of the sunny weather, a cold breeze crept up my naked legs, and the aroma of rain invaded my nostrils. I shuddered and pulled the covers over my head. Did someone open the window on a cold New York autumn day?

In that instant, the faint memories of a dream in which I had slept with a stranger came to me with full force. My stomach made a nervous flip.

What a stupid dream!

The mere possibility of sleeping with someone I didn't know made me wince. I'd never do that. Not in reality. It had to be a dream, because I wasn't the one-night-stand type.

A car honked right outside my window.

I flinched and tried to sit up when a wave of nausea hit me.

Damn!

My head felt as though it had been hit with a sledgehammer. In fact, I had never realized a body could hurt in so many places. Someone had definitely left the windows open, because, while New York City wasn't exactly a place of quietness and serenity, it wasn't usually *that* loud. Groaning, I rolled onto one side and finally pried my eyes open, readying myself to stand and face the noise.

I froze, and for a second, my heart gave out.

Holy shit!

Jett was standing by the open window. My mouth dropped open as I scanned my surroundings. It was definitely my room. And it was definitely him standing there. His gorgeous back was turned to me, and his were hands crossed over his chest as he stared out of the window at the street below. He looked still and reminiscent, but his muscles were tense and matched the emotional undercurrents wafting from him. The light emphasized his naked broad shoulders and rippling muscles. I wondered how long he had been there.

Next to my bed was a bucket that had been cleaned and still glimmered with moisture. Someone had used it, and that someone might have been me. My nausea returned with a vengeance; I was sick to the core at the realization that my lips were swollen, and my abdomen felt deliciously sore. I felt sick as I realized I was naked, and that I might have slept with the stranger. Had I really brought someone home? If so, what was Jett doing in my room, wearing nothing but a pair of dark blue shorts, which praised the fact he was well endowed? I pulled my gaze away from him to my naked breasts.

Oh, God.

Suppressing a groan, I slumped back, fighting the urge to pull the covers back over my head and pray for Earth to swallow me whole. It didn't take a genius to figure out that the stranger hadn't been a stranger at all. Somehow, I had brought my ex back home, even though I had never wanted to sleep with him again—not after he had cheated on me with someone from his past while visiting his brother, who had tried to kill me.

As if sensing my stare, Jett turned around, and my heart skipped a beat. In spite of all the ugly things he had done to me, he was still the most beautiful man I had ever seen. My heart fluttered from his mere presence; all it took was a single glance from him. I stared at his perfect features, inwardly praying for the entire situation to be nothing but a bad dream. But it was indeed Jett: the man who had broken my heart twice. From his green eyes, to his chiseled chest and bulging biceps, to the tribal tattoo covering his left arm and shoulder, he looked like a deadly temptation—an inescapable trap my foolish heart would fall into forever and never escape.

With love comes pain.

"What are you doing here?" I was so shocked that my voice cracked.

"Are you feeling better?" His soft tone reflected his concern. He stepped toward me.

I jumped out of the bed, pressing the cover against my naked body.

"Answer my question, Jett," I hissed. "What are you doing here?"

For a brief moment, confusion crossed his face, and then it turned into a self-assured smile. "We hooked up last night, remember?" He cocked a brow in amusement, and for a second, I could almost feel the pictures flickering before his eyes.

"What do you mean, we hooked up?" I asked, mortified. It was a stupid question, but I had to ask nonetheless, if only to buy myself time to process the obvious.

Seconds ticked by.

"Jett?" *Please say you didn't sleep with me. Please. Please!*

Peering into his face, I knew I was kidding myself; his smile told the entire story.

Just look at his twitching lips, Stewart. He slept with you…and you enjoyed it.

"You asked me to give you a ride home." His voice dripped with insinuation as he regarded me with amusement.

I shook my head. I knew I was in denial, and yet I had to give it a try.

"Does that mean we fucked?" I asked calmly.

The corner of his lips twitched again at my choice of words, and his eyes sparkled with trouble.

"Yes, you could say that." He nodded and inched closer. "You kept calling me your wolf or something. You even begged me for it."

My cheeks caught fire.

"I did what?" I drew a sharp breath and moistened my lips as I tried to make sense of the situation and my strong reaction to him.

His grin widened. "In case you don't remember, I'm happy to refresh your memory. We hooked up, we fucked, and then…we fucked some more." His gaze bored into mine as his lips curled into another heart-dropping smile. "Want to owe me again, *Jenna*?"

Crap. Crap. Crappity crap.

It was official. I had slept with my ex, and I couldn't even blame it on him, because I had begged him to take me. For the first time since meeting Jett, I wished he'd just tell me more lies. And there I had thought I'd be able to move on from him and his hot body without further incident. Then again, he was my first love. No one had ever made me fall so hard or turned me so stupid. No one had made me feel so starved for sex and *him*. I had returned to him before, which was proof that I couldn't trust my own judgment. The fact that I had brought him home again, when I didn't want to, told me that love had made me her bitch and that the only reason I had even considered sleeping with a stranger was because, deep down, I had been looking for a man as attractive as Jett Mayfield. For some reason, I wanted him no matter what. The possibility that I would never be free of my desire to be with him had me fuming.

Anger gripped me—at being so weak, at my heart's fluttering because Jett was in close proximity, at him smelling so good, and at having to force my lips to stop smiling whenever my gaze brushed his hard body.

My blood began to boil in my veins. The attraction to him had to stop. I was so enraged that I grabbed anything I could find, and it so happened to be my high heel. With a cry of frustration, I hurled it at him, but he dodged it, and it hit the wall.

"Why did you say your name was Check?" I shouted, barely able to contain the wrath in my tone.

If he noticed it, he didn't show it. Instead, he let out an amused laugh.

"I thought it was fun that we were playing a game," he said, still wearing that irritating grin of his. "You've always been a sore loser."

"So it was all a game to you? You're so sick and bored of me that you need role play?" I hissed.

His grin disappeared in an instant. He opened his mouth, then closed it again, and a frown began to darken his features.

"You know that's not true, Brooke," he said at last. "You like playing games just as much as I do. It has nothing to do with being bored."

"It has *everything* to do with it." Inside, I felt like a dam was breaking and at any moment water would slush down and flood me. I balled my hands into fists, unable to contain my anger any longer. "I want you out of my life." I grabbed his shirt from the floor and threw it at him. He caught it in midair. "Get out. Get the fuck out of my life."

More confusion crossed his face, followed by dismay, as I took a menacing pace toward him, and shoved him hard.

"It was just a game, Brooke. I was only kidding about you being a sore loser. There's no need to get upset about it."

"It's not about the game. I want you to get out." I pointed to the door in case I hadn't made my point clear enough. "Get out of my life."

It wasn't the elaborate speech I had prepared in my mind, and I sure as hell I didn't mean to shout, but everything inside me was shaking—my voice, my hands, my limbs. At any moment, I was going to explode.

"Brooke..." His tone was gentle and soothing, as though he was talking to a child. "What's going on?" Instead of putting on his damn clothes, he took a step forward.

I flinched. "Stay away from me, Jett."

I held up a hand to prove my point. Jett stared at it with a hard, defiant expression, but he seemed to respect my need for private space.

"Calm down, baby," he said.

Before I could stop him, he stepped toward me and touched my shoulders. I shrugged off his hands, recoiling at the physical contact, even angrier that I wanted him to draw me to him and tell me that we'd be all right.

"Don't you tell me to calm down," I hissed. "I have every right to be angry at you. You played me. If I had known last night that it was you, I never would have slept with you."

He drew in a sharp breath. Shock registered on his face, then disbelief. He looked as if I had just slapped him. In a way, I felt the sharpness of my own words, and it pained me as much as it pained him.

"You thought I was someone else?" he asked in a low tone, his brows drawn in disbelief.

The way he said it, I felt almost threatened.

"Yes," I said through clenched teeth.

"What the fuck, Brooke!"

He released me. Hurt and betrayal shimmered in his eyes. For a second, I felt stunned that I had hit him where it hurt. My heart ached at his pain...until I remembered his betrayal with all its consequences.

"What did you expect, Jett?" I whispered, my voice almost choking me. And there I had been thinking a stranger could make love to me the way Jett had, when it had been him all along, all gorgeous and out of this world. Only, I had forgotten that beauty was an illusion we built inside our heads. The sooner I grasped that and acknowledged it, the faster I'd be able to get away from him.

The silence was deafening, but his answer never came. Instead, he continued to regard me, his gaze betraying his hurt and worry. If I could peer into his soul so easily, then I figured he might at least see the turmoil inside me, and all the things that had crushed my heart, so I turned away, because the magnitude of my love for him had to remain a well-kept secret, or else he could use it against me.

Manipulate me. Tell me what I wanted to hear, even if it wasn't true.

"It's over," I whispered, more to myself than to him. "You can't have me anymore. You can't sleep with me anymore. In fact, I'd rather you just left and never contacted me again."

He let out an annoyed sigh and pushed his fingers through his dark hair just as I had done the previous night when he had pinned me to the floor. "The last time I checked, we were still together."

"Then I am ending things right now." Another sharp pang of pain hit my chest. I turned my gaze to the shaggy rug beneath my feet so I wouldn't have to see his expression. "Can you please leave now?"

As if sensing that I needed space, he walked back to the open window and leaned against the wall, facing me. "I'm not leaving until you tell me what's going on." His voice was calm, but the dangerous undertones didn't escape my attention.

I looked up at him. His face was as hard as stone, and his eyes shimmered with something I couldn't pinpoint. "You know damn right what's going on."

"I actually don't." He pulled his eyebrows together again and let out an annoyed sigh. "Why don't you enlighten me, Brooke?" His hard smile belied his anger.

My pulse began to race, but it wasn't from the physical

attraction that was still palpable in the air. Jett was playing games again, and this time it was the clueless card, but I could see through his pretense—more so because I had seen it coming. The thought that he thought he could lie right to my face infuriated me.

"Damn right, you do," I said through gritted teeth, suppressing the wish to throw something else at him. "I don't trust you as far as I can spit."

He inched closer and grabbed my hand. I drew back before he could pull me to him and before his hard body could envelope me, soothing me the way only Jett knew how.

"Brooke." Another annoyed sigh. "Can you please, for one moment, sit down and explain to me what's going on? The last time you broke things off, you didn't have a freaking choice, but this time? Forgive me for asking, but I'm confused." His voice was hard, his expression detached. I had never seen his stunning green eyes devoid of warmth, and it scared me. His attitude suggested that I was the enemy, as if I was the one causing *him* pain.

"What is there to explain?" I started. "I know."

"What do you know?" He sounded so sincere I laughed bitterly. He wasn't just a good liar; he was an excellent one, who could have probably fooled any lie detector.

I shook my head as I stared him down. "I know *everything*, Jett."

"What do you mean?" He sighed. "What exactly do you *think* you know?"

Now he was turning downright patronizing.

"Fine. If this is the way you want to play." I smiled bitterly. With the sheet still wrapped around me, I sat across from him and ran a hand through my hair. My eyes settled on him in what I hoped was an icy expression. A few seconds passed. I took a deep breath and released it slowly, then continued, a little calmer, "Did you really think I'd still want to date you after I found out you fucked Tiffany?"

He stared at me, shell-shocked, as though I had just dropped a bomb. I had expected to feel better after the confrontation, but I didn't. Instead, all the hurt of being cheated on, of being betrayed, returned full force, multiplied by a million.

"I didn't fuck her," Jett said at last, and paused, choosing his words carefully as he wiped his brow. "Not recently anyway. I mean, it happened a long time ago."

"How long ago?" I asked calmly, but the tremble in my voice betrayed my hurt.

"Last year." His gaze connected with mine, his eyes begging me to understand. "It was before I met you."

He didn't even deny they had been lovers, and a year wasn't as long ago as he made it out to be. Judging from their intimate communication, they still were close. A sudden pang of jealousy pierced my heart.

"Are you still in love with her?"

"What?" He let out an awkward laugh, then stopped, frowning at my hurt reaction. "Is that what this is about? About Ti?" He stared at me in disbelief. "Trust me, Brooke, nothing is going on between us. As I said, it happened a long time ago."

I snorted as I thought back to the incident at the bar: her lips on his, her tongue in his mouth, the insinuation that she had booked a hotel room for them, the fact that he had wanted to see her, and that she had been pregnant by him.

"How do I know you're telling the truth? How can I trust you?" I whispered and stared at him, unable to comprehend that he was lying to my face. My eyes began to sting again. "You saw her behind my back."

"What are you..." His eyes widened as realization kicked in.

"Did you really think I wouldn't find out?" My voice broke.

A short moment passed. For the first time, I noticed that Jett couldn't look at me. He remained silent again, and in some twisted way, that was worse than a whole chorus of lies. A stray tear ran down my cheek. I wiped at it angrily before he could see it.

"So you won't even deny that you kissed her?" I exclaimed, ignoring the sharp stab ripping through my chest.

"I didn't," he whispered.

"Liar." I took a sharp breath and let it out slowly. "Don't you understand, Jett? I was there, right in the same room with you, behind the ice sculpture, watching you both, listening to every word. There's no point in lying. Whatever you have to say, I know the truth."

He wavered as his green gaze pierced me, urging me to open up and trust him.

"I didn't kiss her, Brooke," he said, his tone soft, begging me to understand. "If you were there, then you know that I didn't start it, nor did I want her advances."

I wanted to believe his lies. It would have been easy to sink into his arms and give in to his false assurances, but I was past that. The truth, as shattering as it was, was easier to deal with at that point. I didn't want to be broken anymore. I needed things out in the open so I could finally heal.

"Sure didn't look like it." I laughed bitterly again, but my heart was hurting so much I feared I might just pass out.

"It was all her doing," he said.

Oh, he was good. Too good. I had to give him that. Now he blamed it on Tiffany. "I don't believe you. You're a cheater and a liar."

"Say that again." His tone finally betrayed his anger and irritation. He was slowly losing his composure and patience with me.

"What difference does it make if she started it, or you?" I asked, ignoring the menacing tone in his voice. "You kissed her back and that's all that matters to me."

"Everything, Brooke. *Everything*," he said angrily. "I pushed her away, and do you know why?" He glowered at me. "Because I don't love her. I love *you*. Don't you understand? I love you, Brooke—you and no one else. If you had stayed longer, you would have seen it. You would have heard what I said to her." He moistened his lips, and his tone softened, but his eyes continued to betray his true feelings. "Trust me. It came as a surprise to me that she still cares for me after all this time, but I can't change that. Only she can."

"And that's supposed to make me feel better?" I asked.

"I don't know, but it's the truth, and like I said, I can't change it." His hand reached out for me in a silent urge to let him come close to me again. I stared at it, then blatantly ignored the gesture.

"I don't believe you."

His eyes narrowed, the waves of anger wafting from him almost palpable in the air. I had never seen him that angry before, and it scared me.

He was a dangerous man, just like the rest of his family.

My heart pounded hard in my chest as he inched closer to me, jaw clenched, a vein throbbing in his temple. Towering over me, he was so strong it would have been easy for him to crush me. I flinched as his fingers touched my cheek and trailed down my face to lift my chin. To my surprise, his touch was gentle, almost intimate.

"I would *never* cheat on you," he said. "The thought never even entered my mind." His voice came hard and full of unspoken accusation. "But you?" He pointed a finger at me. "You have no excuse for what you tried to do. You could have called and talked with me before you went off to get drunk and sleep with the next guy." He spat out the words, his eyes ablaze with an anger I had never seen before. "Have you forgotten that we're expecting a baby?" The words were as poisonous as venom, slicing through the frail shell of trust we had built around us.

I opened my mouth to speak, then closed it again, struck speechless by the daggers in his eyes.

"I know that. Trust me, I'm reminded every hour of every day," I whispered bitterly, "and while I know I want this child, I'm not sure I want you as the father. With all your lies and going behind my back, how can I ever trust you again? How can I ever know if you're telling me the truth?"

"Because I do, Brooke," he said through gritted teeth. "It's as simple as that."

For a brief moment, I felt guilty, and then I pushed his hand away. How dare he accuse me while trying to turn himself into a victim when Tiffany wasn't even the only problem? And why was he so angry with me for wanting to move on when he should have been aiming his anger at his ex for kissing him, at his brother...at anything but me?

Come on, what was worse: finding out the one person you trusted was cheating, lying, bonding with a killer, or the possibility of me thinking I was sleeping with a stranger, when it was in fact Jett all along? The question was a no-brainer. He had no right to be angry with me. In fact, he should have seen it coming.

"You're full of shit, Jett." I took a menacing step forward but kept enough distance to jump back in case he decided to put so much as a finger on me. "It's my right to go out and have fun. You betrayed my trust, and I can sleep with whomever I want. You swore you'd never lie to me."

He cut me off. "And I haven't broken that trust."

"Oh, you did," I hissed, narrowing my eyes. "You broke that trust the moment you met with your brother behind my back and kept secrets. Secrets I had every right to know. Why couldn't you just tell me that he's free? That you missed him so much you had to visit him?"

His eyes widened in surprise, and then he blinked, composing himself.

"How do you know—" He stopped midsentence. Wrinkles creased his forehead as he blew a ragged breath. "There's a reasonable explanation for it." He wiped a hand over his face, hesitating, and then his shoulders slumped in defeat. "Look, I get that you're pissed at me, but it's just...complicated. You need to trust me."

I crossed my arms over my chest and regarded him coolly. "Tell me, Jett."

He pressed his lips into a tight line, and my heart sank in my chest. Whatever the explanation was, I knew instantly that he wasn't going to share it with me.

"I can't," he said quietly, his expression softening a little. "I have my reasons. You need to trust me."

"What reasons would that be?"

He clamped his mouth shut.

"Okay." I smiled bitterly. "Tell me just one thing, Jett. Just one. That's all I'm asking for. Did you or did you not log into my account and delete one email related to the estate?"

He shook his head. "I don't think you..."

"Just answer the question." I stared him down, cutting him off. "Did you or did you not?"

"I did." Sighing, he raised his arms in surrender. "But I have a good reason. You..."

My brows shot up as another pang of anger washed over me. "What the hell! Are you controlling me?"

"No, that's not it."

"What other reason would that be?"

"I can't tell you, Brooke. You *have* to trust me."

"I don't have to do anything." The thought that after

everything we had been through he was still keeping secrets from me hurt. My vision blurred with unshed tears of disappointment. "Get out!" I crossed the room in a few steps, then turned around, unable to hide my disgust for him. "The only reason you won't tell me is because you can't come up with a lie that quickly. Don't even pretend otherwise." I opened the door and waited for him to leave.

He shot me a confused look but made no move to leave. Instead, he crossed his arms over his chest and regarded me coolly. "Why would I do that, Brooke?"

There were so many possible reasons I could have thrown at him, but I decided to keep it short and simple.

"I don't know. Maybe because you sided with your brother, and you both want to kill me to get my estate?" The words escaped my lips before I could stop them. It was too late to back off now. "That's the other reason why I wanted to sleep with someone else, so I could move on from you."

He drew in a sharp breath as an array of emotions crossed his beautiful features. Shock. Disbelief. Anger. And then a cold hardness, as though his heart had just turned to ice.

"You thought I wanted to kill you?" he asked slowly, his voice so forceful that I recoiled. "Brooke, are you even listening to yourself?"

I jutted my chin out, standing my ground.

Silence filled the room. Seconds passed. I had never seen Jett so angry. From the way his hands had balled into fists, he looked like he was about to punch a wall. Then again, I had never been so angry myself. What answer could I give him, anyway? That, yes, I had thought he wanted to kill me? That I couldn't trust him and it was over? I tensed when he moved past me. I expected him to touch me again, to utter thousands of excuses. Instead, he grabbed his clothes and turned to leave. Without another word, he walked out, slamming the door behind him, the *thud* reverberating from the walls. I jumped in shock but still didn't move, doing nothing to stop him. It was only when I heard a car door slam outside the window and tires screeching that I knew he was gone.

Out of my life.

Out of my baby's future.

Loud sobs escaped my throat. I sank to the floor and buried my face in my hands. I should have been filled with pure anger, yet buried beneath all those negative feelings for him, there was guilt—for hurting him, for choosing that day to break up, for even giving up on love. My heart was hurting in so many places, and while I hated him, I hated myself more.

The nausea in my stomach intensified by a hundredfold.

Why couldn't I feel anger inside me? Why was I fighting an array of emotions—stupid, stronger feelings that urged me to run after him, to explain the situation, to tell him that he was still the only one for me, that I wanted him more than anything else—even when I resisted in my mind?

I wanted to tell him that, in spite of his cheating, I couldn't stop loving him, and I had no idea why. The last thing I remembered was the awful sickness as I dashed to the bathroom to empty the remnants of my stomach.

Chapter 14

Love is an unpredictable thing. It never listens to you. It doesn't follow your commands. It is like a stubborn cat, eager to chase the next running mouse and to catch it for a trophy. I felt like that mouse, with a sense of ominous, impending doom hanging over my head and no knowledge of which direction to take. I was running in fear, hoping that one day I'd bump into the door that would lead me to freedom, and Jett wouldn't be waiting on the other side, ready to capture me, ready to make me fall for his wicked charm again. With his sexy smile and his green eyes, he had enslaved my body like no other man. I had no wish, no desire, and certainly no need to fall blindly into the next trap, and Jett Mayfield certainly was one.

Our entire relationship had been so intense that I knew it couldn't be healthy for my soul. The moment he had kissed me, I had instantly wanted him, as though my body was programmed to react to him, just as my mind couldn't stop thinking about sex when he wasn't around.

I felt as if I was lost in a dark mausoleum, and he was like the phantom of the opera, shrouded in darkness, with the power to sing to me in my sleep and appear in my dreams. He only had to speak my name in that sexy Southern accent of his, and I would turn to butter in his hands.

I laughed darkly at the comparison of Jett with the phantom; the irony wasn't lost on me. I just hoped I wouldn't end in a straightjacket. After all, my love and desire for him not only turned me blind; it also rendered me insane.

Sitting in bed with my arms wrapped around me, I had absolutely no clue what was going on. Shouldn't he feel some guilty for kissing Tiffany? And why was he so angry anyway? My mind fought to come up with an explanation as to what had gone wrong. Jett hadn't seemed to feel particularly guilty about the fact that I had seen them. Instead, he had been furious. Call it wishful thinking, but I had imagined he'd feel repentant, sorry for all the things he had done, maybe even try to conjure up a bunch of convincing lies. I wouldn't even have been surprised if he had fled the moment a conflict arose, because aren't men supposed to be enemies of difficult chitchats, accusations, and drawn-out drama?

Any sort of reaction would have pleased me more than Jett demanding an explanation and then leaving angry, as if he wasn't to blame and I was the one with the loose screw.

I snorted.

It wasn't at all the Jett I knew—calm and direct. The man who had built one of the most prestigious real estate businesses in the world from scratch. The man who had hardly broken a sweat when racing through the winding roads of Italy's mountains, with pursuers hot on our tail. Yet, the mere thought that I believed I slept with someone other than him—even though, in my mind, it had been just a dream—had hurt and enraged him more than anything. That would have been reasonable if it weren't for the fact that he had met Tiffany behind my back. I could only guess it had been his guilt speaking.

The rage had been etched in his flaming eyes, which morphed into a wildfire when I suggested he might want to kill me to get his hands on the Lucazzone estate.

Oh, my god, the rage—just because I suggested he might want to kill me to get his hands on the estate. I shook my head. It wasn't even *that* farfetched. The news was rife with dark stories of murder and betrayal out of greed. Why wouldn't I assume the worst when his brother was a killer and Jett had been visiting him in prison? He had told me a lie once. I chose to believe him, and he did it again.

It was a perfectly reasonable explanation. It was the only explanation I had, given the fact that Jett had refused to share his reasons for keeping secrets. All he had to do was answer my questions. He refused and begged for undeserved trust instead. The fact that he wouldn't be honest annoyed me; it implied that I was right, strengthening my need to keep my distance from him. He had too much power over me, and I needed a second perspective.

I retrieved my cell phone from the nightstand and texted the only sane person I knew: Sylvie. As her best friend, it was my duty to tell her everything before Jett did. The last thing I needed was for her to side with him. I texted:

You'll never guess what happened last night. I slept with J, and I didn't even know it! I feel like shooting myself. Don't trust him if he calls you. Xx Brooke.

I sent the message, pulled on a baggy sweater that went all the way down to my knees, and then closed the window absent-mindedly. Thousands of thoughts raced through my mind, but they were nothing compared to the millions of feelings threatening to throttle me.

For a while, I stood in front of the window, the weight of the situation lingering heavy in the air. Eventually, I turned my attention toward the apartment building on the other side of the road. In front of it stood a couple with a little boy sitting on top of the man's shoulders. They discussed something for a moment, and then the woman just smiled the kind of smile that signaled happiness. His lips melted into hers in a brief but intimate kiss, as though they were used to public displays of affection. My heart ached at the way she smiled proudly at her little family.

I will never have a family with Jett.

My baby will never know what a real family feels like, never ride atop Daddy's shoulders in the sunshine.

The thoughts sat in the pit of my stomach like heavy rocks. While I had pushed Jett away, a part of me wasn't ready to let him go just yet. That same foolish part of me kept hoping he wouldn't give up on us so easily, wished he'd find a way to prove to me that he was an honest man.

A heavy sadness washed over me at the realization of how much I had believed in our future, how much I had looked forward to raising our child together—as a happy family. Now that it was over, we would be estranged parents, one poor and the other rich and successful. Someday, Jett would find someone else and marry her, and while the thought had been lingering at the back of my mind ever since we met, time hadn't taken the sting out of it.

As I returned to the warmth of my bed, I realized I was still shaking from the fight. Too many things had piled up, but they were nothing compared to the bad feeling of impending doom. Nate was out, and with him free, I had no doubt Jett would be seeing him on a regular basis, just as he had before.

Ignoring Jett's scent on the pillows, I leaned back and began to flick through my messages. The legal firm hadn't replied. For a moment, I considered calling them again, then decided against it. For one, I was a professional and didn't want to seem as though I was harassing them. And then I figured if they thought the matter important, they'd get back to me. I had nothing to lose by waiting a little longer.

My eyes rested on the wallpaper on my cell phone screen, a picture of Jett and me, laughing and grimacing at the camera. A sharp pang shot through my heart as I remembered that day in all its vivid glory. It was one of the many happy memories—too many to count. The first day of autumn, we had been sitting in the park, fooling around, capturing both the change in seasons and our blossoming love. Or at least *my* blossoming love. Not his. He was probably too busy thinking about screwing his ex.

Before I could change my mind, I deleted the picture and replaced the wallpaper with the image of a desolate winter landscape in the hope that the loneliness would empty my mind and the snow would gradually freeze over my feelings.

Chapter 15

By midday, the entrance door opened, and footsteps thudded across the corridor. My pulse spiked, but there was no time to steady my nerves or hide. I knew it was my best friend. The way she hurried in, I almost expected her to shout, "*Fire.*"

Sylvie threw open the door, her first question hitting me before she even set foot in the room. "Please tell me I've been pranked, because someone just texted me that you slept with Jett."

Her blonde hair was a mess, and her cheeks were flushed, as if she had been running a couple of blocks, which couldn't be, because Sylvie never engaged in physical activity of any kind, unless it was to get a limited edition of shoes at half-price. I sat up and regarded her grimly as she sat on the edge of the bed, barely able to move in her fluffy, pink cashmere sweater, tight red pants, and dark brown high heels. In spite of her flushed face, she looked as if she had just stepped off a runway.

"I wish," I muttered, "just as much as I wish I could kill myself this instant." To my horror, a tear ran down my face.

"*Oh my God*," Sylvie exclaimed in shock. "You didn't!" Slowly, she shook her head in what I assumed was exasperation; that was understandable as I, too, was slowly growing exasperated with myself. "Why would you do that?"

Why indeed?

"Because I didn't know it was him." I raised my hand in defense, feeling defeated.

Her eyes widened. "But how...*how* could you not know it was Jett?"

"I don't know." I raised my hand in defense, feeling defeated. "And before you ask, no, I've no idea how I couldn't know. I just didn't recognize him. It all happened so fast. It was dark and the lights in the club made him look strange and distorted." The whole thing rang farfetched, unbelievable, because it was.

"But still. You have ears. You must have spoken at some point and yet you didn't recognize his voice?" Sylvie asked in disbelief, her tone dripping with accusation.

Talk about not being judgmental! What happened to compassion?

"There is a term for it," I muttered. "It's called selective perception, seeing and hearing only what your mind chooses to see and hear. Google it if you don't believe me."

"I might do that," Sylvie said and plopped down on the edge of the bed. "What was he doing at the club anyway?"

"I've got no idea." That was the one question I didn't get the chance to ask.

She shook her head in disbelief again. "Jesus, Brooke. I thought we talked about this." She kicked off her expensive shoes, exposing swollen feet and red, painful marks that would soon turn into blisters. "Don't you remember what you've been drilling into me for years?" She cocked an eyebrow meaningfully.

I shook my head to signal that I had no clue.

She picked up her left shoe and held it up in the air like a preacher waving a Bible around. "If a shoe doesn't fit the first time you try it on, it'll always give you blisters. Why don't you trust your own advice and accept that if a man hurts you once, he will always hurt you?"

Her footwear analogy summoned a faint smile to my lips. "Jett isn't your average pair of shoes," I retorted. "He's a big, fat gumboot and too much to handle. Nothing gets to him. Nothing can change his form. He does what he wants, whenever he wants, and how he wants it, paying no mind to anyone else's feelings. I'm swimming in those shoes, but I can't seem to pull them off." Hysteria bubbled in the back of my throat. I turned to Sylvie in the hopes she'd get the joke, but worry was still etched into the lines of her face.

"I'm serious, Brooke." Her frown deepened. "A shoe is a shoe, and if it doesn't fit the first time you try it on, it never will. There are no exceptions."

My laughter died in my throat. I let out a sigh and nodded. She had always looked out for me, and as much as I would have preferred otherwise, she was right. No matter how hard I tried to deny it, Jett wasn't good for me. I might have adjusted to his ways, but that didn't mean I wouldn't have to endure all sorts of pain along the way, unless I gave up on us forever.

"You're right. I'm sorry." I relented. "I know I shouldn't have slept with him. It's just…" I struggled for words.

How could I possibly explain to her that, on a subconscious level, my body responded to him because I loved him? That it didn't matter if Jett wore a paper bag on his head, that something inexplicable kept pulling me to him. I couldn't change that, whether I wanted it or not.

Sylvie's face lit up.

"I know what went wrong," she said coolly. "You had to be drunk, because no woman in her right mind would ever take back a guy like him after the stunt he pulled."

What she didn't realize was that I very well might not have been in my right mind. All rational thought had flown out the door the moment Jett entered my life.

I pressed the pillow against my chest as I recalled the previous months' events. Even when I knew I shouldn't trust a guy with a Southern accent, gorgeous lips, and a body to die for, my brain had switched off at the mere sight of him. His charm and looks had persuaded me to jump into bed with him soon after we met. I had let my guard down and allowed myself to fall in love with him.

Fighting the urge to explain, I gave a careless shrug. It would have been much easier to let Sylvie think the influence of alcohol was to blame. But, for some reason, I just couldn't.

"You know me," I said. "I don't get drunk easily. I had one drink, two max. That's it. I swear."

"I knew it. You would never let a guy like Jett back into your bed under normal circumstances." In spite of her stern voice, a gentle smile lit up her face as she regarded me. "You know your Jersey-Shore-partying days are over. As much as you love to party, you can't do that anymore, not in your condition."

I rolled my eyes. Sylvie was worse than my mother. Not only was she trying to see straight through me, but she also always managed to make me feel worse. My previous life couldn't have been more different. It had all been about work and building a career that had gone nowhere—until Jett entered my life and offered me a job with Mayfield Realties.

"You're right," I replied, unconvinced. "I should give up on fun altogether."

"That's not what I meant. But drinking yourself into a stupor so you didn't even recognize the devil? That's…"

Figuring that Sylvie would go on for a while, I stopped listening. As I crossed my legs on the bed, I noticed a blue bruise on my thigh, and I realized it must have happened when I stumbled. Fuzzy images began to flood my mind.

Even though I hadn't realized it was him, Jett had managed to break my fall. I remembered the way the stranger had held me, his arms wrapped around my waist, his hot breath on my face as he said something I couldn't remember. While I knew for a fact that I had barely had one and a half cocktails and the alcohol might have wreaked havoc on my body, was it enough to make me believe I was in a dream and cause trouble remembering specific details such as the events after my fall?

Possibly.

However, not likely.

And why had I kept seeing a wolf? It must have been some kind of hallucination, brought on by Jett's intimidating flair.

The question that bothered me the most was why spin a

concoction of phantasms rather than just recognize Jett? Sylvie was right: Even under the influence of alcohol, that part made no sense.

I closed my eyes, because I couldn't believe what I was about to say. "Jett asked if I was high. It didn't strike me as odd at the time, but now…" I opened my eyes. My gaze scanned the room before settling on the bucket, and a horrible thought crossed my mind.

Sylvie spoke out the obvious first. "You think your drink was spiked?" she asked, narrowing her eyes. I grimaced but didn't respond. "Do you think he would—"

I shook my head, horrified at the thought. "No. That wasn't Jett. Gina bought all the drinks." I paused long enough to notice Sylvie's frown, then added, "She's someone I met at work."

"I see," Sylvie said, deep in thought.

I didn't like the look on her face and almost feared what she'd say next, but to my surprise, she just leaned back on the bed for a minute.

"Back when we were in college, my mom always had that irrational fear that we'd get into drugs, remember?" Sylvia finally said.

I nodded, unsure of where she was going.

"It didn't exactly help that some guy smoked pot in the communal kitchen right before my mom popped in for a surprise visit," Sylvie continued.

I grinned, remembering the scene vividly. Her mother had been livid, and back then, I was sure I'd never see Sylvie again. She never told me how she managed to diffuse that bomb.

"She bought a couple home drug-testing kits to detect the presence of common street and prescription drugs— you know, the usual, like ecstasy, amphetamines, opiates, and that stuff."

"Really?" I stared at her, open-mouthed. "I didn't even know they make such a thing. No wonder you never told me."

Sylvie waved her hand, her expression betraying her annoyance. "Wait, that's not all. Whenever she made one of her surprise visits, which was often, she insisted that I do the test. If I refused she'd cut off my allowance." She grimaced, and her expression darkened just a little more. "Anyway, my point is that the test is 99.9 percent accurate. Were it not for the negative results, my mom never would have believed I wasn't taking anything because she has this unnerving tendency not to trust anyone, including her own daughter."

"Wow. Your mom…" I shook my head in disbelief. "I don't blame her for what she did though. We used to party pretty hard."

"Yeah, like crazy." Sylvie let out a high laugh as her expression adopted that faraway look that screamed she was being transported back to a different time in our lives. "Anyway, I still have a kit in my room. If you unknowingly took any drugs in the past forty-eight hours, we can know for sure within a few minutes. So..." She looked at me, surveying me for a moment. "Are you up for it?"

"What? Now?"

"Yeah, now." She jumped up and pulled me to my feet. "It's probably expired, but we could still give it a shot."

I nodded, even though the idea wasn't exactly appealing. How would I react if the test came back positive? What could I possibly assume other than that Gina might be into drugs and that she might have thought she was doing me a favor, helping me loosen up? It wasn't unusual or unheard of. I had grown up in an area where teens offered others drugs, because they assumed their friends wanted to give them a try, too. But would Gina do that without even asking me? I just couldn't believe she'd sneak it on me, without even telling me.

I watched as Sylvie retrieved a box from an upper shelf in her bedroom and motioned for me to follow her. Even as I walked after her, I knew I didn't want to go through with the test because I feared its outcome. Then again, if I didn't find out, the fear of *not* knowing would always be greater, nagging at the back of my mind. Metaphorical dark clouds descended upon me as soon as I joined Sylvie in the bathroom. For some reason, it was almost as bad as peeing on a pregnancy test. With each passing second, I grew more anxious, and finally it was time to evaluate the results.

"Here you go," Sylvie said.

With a flick of her hand, I had my answer. We both stared at the paper in shock. All substances appeared to be negative, except one.

What the hell!

"You're positive for GHP," she whispered.

"Now would be a great time to shoot me," I murmured. Sylvie opened her mouth to protest or lecture me, but I held up my hand to stop her. "Don't. I don't want to hear it."

"I'm sorry," Sylvie said slowly.

"Don't be." I looked at her grimly, my mind strangely devoid of thoughts. I should have been shocked, fuming mad about the results, anything but—cold and composed.

Someone had spiked my drink, and it seemed that someone was Gina, for whatever reason. The comprehension stung, but it didn't register. Instead, something else seemed to take center spot in my mind. The knowledge that I wasn't to blame for what had happened the previous night didn't ease the guilt of having slept with Jett. Perhaps my foggy mind had failed to recognize him and I had mistaken the entire sordid encounter for a dream, but as sure as hell, Jett had been lingering in my memories the whole time. I wanted him, and he was the one I would always want, the choice I would always make, no matter how bad for me.

"Don't be so hard on yourself. It's not your fault, Brooke," Sylvie whispered.

I shook my head, because she didn't understand. It *was* my fault, and I had no one else to blame. "I could have chosen any man. Why him?" I turned away to hide the telltale moisture in my eyes, but I could feel Sylvie's intense gaze burning a hole in my back, and her thoughts and anger were almost palpable in the air.

"Oh, sweetie, come here." She enveloped me in a hug as tears began to trickle down my face again.

Chapter 16

In spite of my constant assurance that I was okay, Sylvie called in sick at work so she could stay with me. She made breakfast for us, consisting of her usual black coffee and toast, then cleared out a box of old movies for us to watch. For the first time in my life, she even offered to cook us Chinese.

I laughed, until her offended expression told me she was being serious.

"We'd better use them before they expire," she said, standing in the kitchen with a brand new apron tied around her narrow waist. Scattered across the table were the contents of a gift box consisting of a cooking set for beginners, complete with Chinese ingredients. She had received it last Christmas from an aunt and had stashed it away in the back of a cupboard, along with all the other clutter she didn't need. At that time, she had claimed the gift was ridiculous. Now, she seemed hell-bent on giving it a try.

I lifted the recipe book and flicked through the first few pages. It was the smallest cookbook I had ever seen, barely bigger than my palm.

"This is it." Sylvie pointed to a page.

Doubting the sanity of her idea, I scanned the recipe and was about to express my concern, when Sylvie opened a packet of black, shriveled fungi. I pinched my nose at the pungent smell: a noxious mixture of old cheese, stale beer, and wasted onions and garlic. "You sure you want to do this?" I asked, even though I knew she wasn't; I could tell from the darting eye movement and the nervousness reflected in her expression. Like me, Sylvie was scared of cooking. "I mean, I appreciate the effort, but we could always just order in." I made it sound nonchalant, as though it didn't matter to me either way, even though I was almost ready to beg her to throw away the smelly stuff and leave the cooking to people who knew what they were doing.

"No." She shook her head with the kind of determination I had learned to fear from her. "I want to cook for you, to do something nice. Anything that makes you feel better, you know?"

My mouth went dry. Usually, when Sylvie tried to do something nice for me, it ended in disaster, but I couldn't bear to tell her that. In order to prevent any calamity that could possibly happen, I would just have to keep an eye on her. "In that case, at least let me help you." I grabbed a knife, ready to chop a carrot, but Sylvie snatched it out of my hands, shooting me an awkward look.

"I'd rather you enjoy the movie." She stashed the knife out of my reach.

Was that a hint of nervousness I detected? I eyed her carefully. Avoiding my probing gaze, she held the knife close to her chest, as if it was some prized possession and anytime someone might try to steal it from her.

My stomach churned.

Surely…no, it couldn't be. As if sensing my stare, her grip around the knife tightened, until her knuckles whitened.

Oh, for crying out loud.

"You're right. I should relax more and take it easy." I smiled. "I'm going to take a bath." I headed for my room and closed the door behind me. I had barely pressed my back against the wall when footsteps thudded down the hall and the door was thrown open. Sylvie's frantic gaze swept over me and then the bathroom. She looked so miserable, that I had to stifle a laugh.

"Taking a bath sounds great, but could you leave the door open? Please?" She smiled but it looked pasted on. "In case I need you," she added. "Thanks." She smiled again and, without another word, she returned to the kitchen.

Oh, my god.

No way. No freaking way.

Sylvie thought I was suicidal. Under different circumstances, I would have laughed and called her out on it. But I couldn't this time because I had no one but myself to blame. Obviously, she had mistaken my joke about killing myself as a call for help. Or maybe I looked like a loose cannon that might go off at any time. I snorted.

As if I would kill myself over Jett.

I opened several doors in our bathroom and scanned the contents of the shelves in the medicine cabinet: pills, razors, and even the hair straightener were gone. Even the belt of my bathrobe was absent. That was ridiculous.

"Sylvie!" I yelled and followed her into the kitchen, unsure if I should be angry or laugh about the absurdity of the situation. "Where's my hair straightener?" Or any other electrical items I might choose to electrocute myself?

"It's…" Sylvie paused, struggling for words. "Faulty. I had to send it back for repairs."

"Really?" I raised my eyebrows. "And where are the razors, so I can shave my legs? I have to be at work at seven."

"Used them." This time, her lie came out smooth and prepared. She even nodded convincingly.

"The whole pack?"

"Yes." Not even a blink.

I opened our utility drawer. All plastic bags were gone. As if I would pull one over my head and suffocate myself. I took a deep breath and released it slowly.

"You wouldn't, by any chance, happen to think I might want to kill myself just because I slept with Jett, would you?" I asked nonchalantly.

Sylvie's eyes popped wide open. She opened her mouth to speak, then closed it, only to reopen it a second later. I held up a hand to stop her.

"I see your point," I said through gritted teeth. "You're afraid I might harm myself, and I appreciate your concern. But—" I heaved an annoyed sigh. "It's not going to happen. I won't kill myself over Jett. Even with all the bad things in my life, that thought has never crossed my mind."

"It's just..." She trailed off, leaving the rest hanging heavy in the air.

"I slept with him, and I know that's a reason for concern." I nodded slowly, trying to keep my voice calm. "I'm reminded of that every hour. And it doesn't exactly help that I still love him or that I was under the influence of drugs without even knowing it. But that doesn't mean I'm suicidal, all right? So, for the sake of my sanity, can you please return my things?"

Sylvie just stared at me.

I frowned. "What?"

"I don't understand, Brooke," she said slowly. "How can you still love him after everything he's done?"

I opened my mouth to offer some sort of witty reply, but my brain failed to come up with any worthy retort. In all the frenzy of her worrying and my assurances that she didn't have to worry about me, the words had just stumbled out of my mouth. Not once had I stopped to think about what I was saying.

Crap!

Why did I have to declare my undying love for him? Even if it was true—truly, crappy, painfully true—Sylvie wouldn't understand. After Jett's angry departure, I had thought hard about him. It wasn't just the images of him and Tiffany and visiting his killer brother that were branded in my mind. I also remembered the hours I had spent with him, all those good times that had made me believe our relationship was long-term material. Even now that it was over, I still thought about him nonstop. Seeing his face in my mind was painful, but so was the fact that I still loved him without wanting to, and there was nothing I could do about that. He was in my mind, behind every thought, every word—sneaking around like the shadow of a draft, always there but not visible to the eye.

"Brooke?" Sylvie prompted. Realizing she was still waiting for an answer, I looked up and grimaced. Of course she wouldn't let it go. For once, couldn't she pretend she didn't hear my foolish declaration of love to the one guy who didn't deserve it?

"There is no off switch to make my heart complete, okay?" I snapped at her. "I thought that seeing his cheating with my own eyes would make me stop loving him. I thought all the pain and anger would erase my feelings for him." I smirked. "But I was wrong. I still love him, and I can't help it. You don't like it. Well, I don't like it either, but you know what? I can't do anything about it." To avoid her pitiful stare, I looked around and began to open drawers. "Where are my things anyway?"

"Uh-uh. I'll never tell you." She shook her head in what I assumed was mock disapproval. "According to various websites, I can't leave you unsupervised with anything you might use to hurt yourself, not until I'm sure you're over him."

I snorted. "You Googled *that*?" I stared at her in disbelief. "Sylvie, I'm fine. No need to panic or turn my hair straightener into contraband."

"People in forums warn that the person might be lying, pretending to be fine to mask the pain until they are alone."

The masking part was true, but I certainly didn't feel suicidal. "Do I look like I'm being irresponsible and ready to kill myself and leave you and my mother behind?" I snapped.

"No, but…" She hesitated.

"Then cut the bullshit." I held out my hand. "My stuff, Sylvie. Please?"

She shook her head again.

I dropped my hand in mock annoyance. "Fine. Whatever. I'll find it myself." With one last glare at her, I headed for her bedroom, but Sylvie blocked my path.

I narrowed my eyes at her and then it dawned on me. She had stashed it all in there.

"I will return everything, under one condition." She held up a manicured index finger.

"Which is?"

"You let me help you."

I let out a short, irritated laugh. "I mean it, Sylvie. You don't have to worry about me harming myself—or him," I said sourly, deliberately avoiding saying Jett's name. I knew I sounded bitter, but my emotions threatened to choke me. "I can accept my feelings for him and yet still not want to be with him. For that, I don't need anyone's help."

"I hope so." The doubt in her tone signaled that she wasn't convinced. "Because if you don't get over him, I'll personally drag your ass to the best LAA group meeting in town."

I raised my eyebrows in confusion. "LAA?"

"Love Addicts Anonymous," she clarified. "If an intervention doesn't help, LAA will solve any sort of obsession problem with any guy."

I rolled my eyes. "I'm *not* obsessed with anyone." In fact, I hated the sound of the word. Even though I had no doubt that LAA existed, the idea of joining some help organization and talking about Jett, then having to listen to other sob stories, was absurd.

"If you say so." Sylvie shot me a skeptical look. "You know, it wouldn't hurt to give it a try."

A pang of annoyance hit me at the realization that Sylvie didn't believe me. Just because I was in love didn't mean I was also obsessed.

Okay, maybe a little.

Still, Sylvie didn't have to be so brutally honest about it.

Disappointment or not, what was wrong with being a little obsessed with the man you loved, thinking about him day and night—which was the result of a bruised ego and hopes that were destroyed?

"I don't owe you an explanation, okay?" My voice trembled slightly as I glared at her. "I might still be in love with Jett, but I'm not crazy, and I'm certainly not bordering on obsessive or jumping-off-a-cliff-compulsive. It would take a lot more to make me jump off a bridge or start stalking him."

"I'm just trying to help," Sylvie said defensively. "I don't want you to get hurt and make the same mistake again."

I wanted to point out I had repeated the mistake before and survived, but I kept my mouth shut.

"No man is worth the pain or waiting for him to change," she continued. "It's easy to be in love with the idea of love rather than actually loving a person."

God, Sylvie could be irritating sometimes.

"You've got it wrong. I'm not in love with the idea of love," I said in a low tone. I sounded so defensive it was almost laughable. "If I were in love with the idea, we'd be married by now, probably horseback-riding on the beach."

She shrugged, unconvinced. "If you say so."

I glowered at her as I began to massage my temples to get rid of the pounding behind them. It wasn't like me to be rude, but Sylvie didn't see how much I wanted to be alone in the dark abyss of my mind so that I could ignore the annoying agony in my chest.

"Maybe you moved in with him too soon," she murmured, oblivious to my reluctance to talk.

For a second, I was taken aback, and my head snapped in her direction. "What do you mean?" I asked, shocked. I had feared the same thing, but I had discarded it. To hear my hidden fear coming from her mouth was daunting.

"Think, Brooke. You did everything *he* wanted. You moved in with him. You worked for him. You always played by his rules." She counted more reasons, but I stopped listening.

The blood in my ears rushed faster, drowning out everything else.

Was it possible that Jett and I had spent too much time together and our relationship fell into a routine, where he felt he didn't have to chase me anymore because he already had me?

My heart lurched at the thought that our relationship had become too boring for Jett. It certainly made sense and explained why he had wanted me to dress up as someone he had never met before. I wasn't a prude when it came to spicing up one's love life and role-playing could be a part of that, but so early in a relationship?

I buried my face in my hands, letting my shoulders drop. "I'm so fucking stupid. I should have moved out as soon as Nate was arrested. Better yet, I never should have moved in with him in the first place."

"It's just a theory, Brooke. I'm not saying it's true. I'm just pleading with you to open your eyes and see him the way I do, rather than loving him for what he appears to be."

It made sense. I had given too much too soon. Sylvie was right. The possibility existed that my obsession with Jett was not only stupid, but in vain, too.

"You've made your point, loud and clear. Now, can you please shut up and leave me alone?" I walked back into the bathroom and slammed the door shut before sinking to the floor, feeling number from the cold than ever before.

Chapter 17

A soft knock carried over from the door.

"Brooke?" Sylvie's voice was filled with worry. A second later, her head appeared in the doorway, and I looked up.

"Yeah?"

"I made us coffee. Are you coming?"

On the heels of anger came acceptance. There was no point in evading her.

Sighing, I stood and walked back into the kitchen and sat down at the table. Sylvie slumped into the seat opposite me and pulled her knees up to her chest, regarding me.

"I want my things back before I go to work," I said, her gaze unnerving me.

"Fine."

For a long moment, Sylvie just stared at me, the oppressing silence heavy with words unspoken. Each passing second frayed my nerves. The way she just sat there, with her arms crossed over her chest and her lips pressed in a tight line, she looked scarier than a scolding schoolteacher. For an awful moment, I feared she might resume her lecture on obsession. The skin on my face prickled. Without intending to, I brushed a hand over my mouth, realizing I had been stroking my abdomen for the past few minutes, the gesture both protective and indicative of my frightening isolation.

Finally, Sylvie sighed and leaned back in her seat, the tension between us slowly dissipating as she watched my movement. "Can you feel the baby?"

"Not yet." I shook my head, relaxing a little, happy for the change in topic. "It will be a while before it starts kicking, but I do feel different. I feel like part of J—" I bit my lip, stopping myself from saying the one thing that kept burning inside my mind. "I feel like something else is inside me."

Sylvie regarded me intently, her expression hardening again, but she didn't probe.

Dammit.

Not only was I under his spell, but I was also having a hard time controlling what came out of my mouth around

Sylvie. No wonder she thought I was in desperate need of an LAA session. After admitting that I still loved him and now proclaiming that he had become a part of me through our unborn child, it was as if I still harbored the slightest hope we would end up together...even though I knew I was kidding myself.

Ending together was impossible. I had broken things off, and he had left me. We were over, even if I couldn't believe it yet.

"I have something for you." She retrieved a yellow envelope from one of the drawers and pushed it into my hands. "I meant to give it to you in a few weeks, but I thought why wait that long?" She shrugged, as though it wasn't a big deal. "I thought we might attend...together."

"What is it?" I opened the envelope but didn't peer inside.

Sylvie raised her eyebrows, urging me to take a look. I did as requested. It was a voucher for childbirth classes. I smiled, suddenly overwhelmed by emotion.

"These will be great. I hadn't even thought of it." It was a kind gesture, and probably one of Sylvie's attempts to try to distract my mind from Jett and help me focus on the future.

"Thank you." I looked up at her. To my surprise, Sylvie didn't return my smile as she watched me push the voucher back inside the envelope, and I couldn't help but feel uneasy. The tension in her posture was unmistakable.

Was that a hint of nervousness on her face?

"Can I ask you something?" she said at last.

I narrowed my eyes, suddenly wary of her scary expression. I wasn't sure how to reply. I didn't want her to ask me anything, but I just said, very carefully, "What?"

"Don't take this the wrong way," she started.

I winced at what might be coming. Sylvie's questions and statements always had that effect on me.

"I know you haven't told your mom about your pregnancy yet. I probably wouldn't either, because she can be a real dragon. But—" She moistened her lips, pausing as she considered her next words. "For the past few weeks, I've been wondering why you don't really make any plans? I'm your best friend, and yet you never talk about the baby. No offense, Brooke, but it would be hard to believe you're three months pregnant, if it weren't for the test."

So it was a personal issue between friends. I relaxed a little.

"Oh, that," I said, flicking my wrist.

It was true.

Up until that moment, I had always avoided any discussion about the baby. I didn't talk about my pregnancy like other expecting women, and I understood why it was a matter of concern for Sylvie. The truth was, even though I had listened and gone along with Jett's and Sylvie's suggestions, the entire situation seemed surreal. Now that Jett and I were over, I was trying even harder to banish any thoughts of what the future might have in store.

I smirked. "I'm not like other people, Sylvie. Maybe others want to scream it at the top of their lungs, but I don't. I'm not comfortable telling the whole world my business."

"But why? Aren't you excited?" She narrowed her eyes. "Just because you and he are over, it shouldn't change anything. You should be proud, go shopping, plan a baby shower. You should be talking about it nonstop, you know, do all the stuff women do when they're pregnant. I'd love to help, even though I'm not even keen on having kids." She paused, eyeing me cautiously. "Is it because of Jett?"

I winced inwardly at the way she said his name, as if he resembled an infectious disease.

"No. It's—" My voice failed me. I took a deep breath and released it slowly. "It has *nothing* to do with him."

I shot her a begging look, silently urging her to stop talking about him. Couldn't she leave the matter be, forget his name like I was trying to?

"What is it then?" Sylvie insisted.

"It's just...I can't believe that I'm pregnant."

"So being in denial is your solution?" She stared at me in shock. "You have to face reality eventually, particularly when you stop fitting into your clothes."

"I'm *not* in denial," I protested. "I just don't want to risk anything."

"Risk? I don't understand." She spread her hands, palms out, her usually smooth forehead creased in a frown. "What's the problem? I understand you don't want to talk about Jett, but what about your baby?"

"You're a hell of annoying, you know that?" I laughed, even though the situation didn't seem particularly amusing to me.

"I'm your friend. I'm supposed to be annoying." She leaned forward, smoothing her hair back. "That's what friends are for. We're supposed to breathe down your neck to make sure you stay on track, but I can't do that if you keep things to yourself. Ever since you met Jett, you've been shutting me out. Have you ever thought about how that makes me feel?" Her tone betrayed her hurt.

Surprised, I looked up at her and slowly realized that Sylvie had likely felt that way for a while. Shame burned through me.

Had I been so blind that I didn't realize I was neglecting our friendship? We had been friends forever, and yet there were things Sylvie still didn't know about me—things only Jett knew. For the past few weeks, I had been so focused on Jett that I had not realized Sylvie might feel left out. She had always been the sister I lost. And now with Jett gone, she was all I had. There was no doubt that she deserved my trust more than he did. I owed it to her to tell the truth.

"Look, I get your concern." I sighed. "I know it's wrong not to talk about things, but if I start talking, I'll start making plans. I'll dream and hope, and I don't want to do that right now. When I was with Jett, I always had this unexplained fear that something would happen."

"That you would break up?" Sylvie cut in. The question was harmless enough.

"No. It wasn't only that," I said softly.

I walked over to the coffeemaker. We had been so engrossed in our discussion that she had forgotten to switch it off. I poured steaming coffee in two cups, then handed Sylvie hers.

"I want this child more than anything, but I don't want my hopes raised, only to see them shattered," I said. "What's so wrong with that? If you had experienced what I've gone through, you'd probably feel the same way." I wrapped my fingers around the cup, but even the hot liquid didn't warm my cold hands. Looking up into Sylvie's blue eyes, I remembered it wasn't that long ago that someone had planned to kill me.

Sylvie remained quiet, so I continued, "Trust me, I *want* to embrace motherhood. I *want* to paint the nursery in hues of pink and blue. I want to talk about baby plans all day, but I can't. Do you understand?" I paused, wondering whether the question was directed at myself as much as at Sylvie.

"It's just not an option at the moment—not when Nate is free and I'm living in constant fear. Every night is a struggle, and I can't fall asleep. I'm in such a state, I don't dare hope for the better, and I most certainly don't imagine what things could be like."

I waited for Sylvie to ask another question, but she remained uncharacteristically silent. With a frown, she stared at her coffee, engrossed in her own thoughts.

"I understand," she whispered at last. "I'm sorry, Brooke. I was so wrapped up in the belief that you weren't happy about being pregnant that I thought..." She stopped in thought, unable or unwilling to finish her sentence.

"It's okay. I know you mean well," I said softly, my hand starting to rub my flat tummy, a habit I had developed since I'd learned I was pregnant.

Please stop talking about my baby or Jett. Especially Jett.

"Anyway, let's not linger on those depressing issues." I forced a smile onto my lips, even though there was no feeling behind it. "Enough about me already. What about you? What are your plans for the day?"

As if sensing my need for a change in topic, Sylvie lifted a mushroom and smelled it, then grimaced. "I'm going on a date today."

"What?" I said, agog. "With whom? Why didn't you tell me sooner? We could have gone shopping to find you a nice dress."

She smiled with little enthusiasm and shrugged. "It's no big deal. A friend set me up on a blind date. I might call it off." Sylvie loved going on dates, and more than anything, she loved any excuse to go shopping. It was odd for her not to be excited about it.

I inched next to her, knowing that the only reason she'd blow one off was because she thought I needed her.

"No, you should definitely go," I said. "In fact, I insist. Just because I'm having a bad day doesn't mean you have to stay home and play babysitter. Besides, I'm working late today."

"I don't know." She hesitated, catching my eyes. "Will you be okay?"

I smiled gently and shrugged. "Sure I will. You've already helped me so much."

It was the truth. Sylvie and I might have had our conflicts and our own personal dramas, but having her near me, knowing she cared so much about me, helped me. I had always admired Sylvie, with good reason. She had gone through many more breakups than I had, and yet she was quick to stand up and move on. It was as if her heart was free to love whomever she wanted, and she could easily let go with the prospect of dating the next guy, whereas I just wouldn't learn from my mistakes.

My heart resembled a trained falcon with its feet tied to its master and a hood on its head, unable to escape into freedom. All my life, I had vowed that I would never let anyone into my heart. When I made an exception for Jett, I never thought that it would change my life. My priorities and focus had shifted to the point that I had neglected my friends and my mother. My plans had been put on the back burner, and previous goals had lost importance. Too many things had changed, me included.

Sitting in the silence, in our old kitchen, with the penetrating ticking of the old clock above the door as the only sound, I realized that while I couldn't turn back time, I still had the power to change things to how they used to be. Having Sylvie close reminded me why I had to stick to my resolutions and promises never to let a man control my heart.

"You go on your date," I said resolutely. "I'll even help you choose a dress."

"If you insist." She smiled at me. "But you've got to give me a hand with this cooking."

"Are you really going to cook those things?" I pointed to the mushrooms in her hand, my mortification probably written all over my face. I was standing a few feet away, yet I could still smell the unpleasant bouquet of hippie, old cheese, and gym socks. I hoped the stench would dissipate, because I wasn't going to eat anything smelly. Besides, they looked so dark and wrinkled, I doubted they were edible at all.

Even Sylvie looked doubtful as she eyed the old mushrooms with the kind of disgusted expression she usually reserved for spiders or anything that had more than four legs, but she remained quiet.

"Not trying to say I don't want you to do something nice for me, but maybe we could do Chinese another day? I'd kill for a pizza with cheese crust, pepperoni, onions, and black olives," I said. "What do you think?"

"Thank God. Me too." She looked genuinely relieved as she dropped the shriveled mushrooms. "I'd love ham and extra cheese. With lots of different toppings, right? I can wolf that stuff down like no other."

I beamed at her. "Same as always."

God, I loved Sylvie.

My gaze followed her as she got up and crossed the room. She was almost out the door when I called out, "Sylvie?"

She stopped and turned around. "Yeah?"

"Thank you," I whispered. "You're such a good friend. I have no idea what I'd do without you."

A mysterious smile lit up her glossy lips. "I'm not a good friend." I frowned and she let out a soft laugh. "A good friend knows about your best days, but a best friend has lived through all your worst. See the difference?" she whispered. "I'm your *best* friend, Brooke. Guys will come and go and break you in pieces, but I will always be here to mend you again."

"Then you're my Super Glue," I said, laughing.

"Damn right I am." She flashed another smile and picked up the phone to order our lunch.

Chapter 18

The whole day passed in a blur. Sylvie tried to distract me with movies and food, but I constantly found myself checking my phone like an obsessive lunatic. Jett didn't contact me. No calls. No messages. Nothing to indicate that he wanted to work things out. His indifference was a blessing and helped to put things in perspective, but even though I should have been thankful, it bothered me.

The more I pored over Sylvie's words, the more I wondered what Jett had been doing at the club and what had stopped him from telling me the truth, and, of course, why my foolish brain couldn't stop thinking about him. I cursed my weakness for him. Hour after hour, I wished my feelings for him far away, and they kept crawling back like ants to sweets.

I wanted to forget him, but at the same time, I wanted to hear from him. I wanted to see him in pain while wishing him nothing but the best. So many conflicting emotions twisted into an ever-present knot of contradiction and impatience.

I had to get a grip. And fast, before my life stopped belonging to me, and Jett became the sole focus of my attention.

At 6:45 p.m., Thalia picked me up from around the corner, the same place where she'd dropped me off before, and we made our way to Grayson's studio. From the corner of my eyes, I glanced at her gorgeous, yellow, lacy dress, complete with stockings and black high heels. Her glossy, long hair was tied up in a complicated burlesque hairstyle, with beautifully defined curls and waves added to the sides and front, complementing her pretty face.

Something wafted from her, an air of confidence that brushed over me and made me feel different. I took a deep breath and let it out slowly as I allowed her enthusiasm and congeniality to wash over me and make me feel at ease. Listening to her chatter, I actually looked forward to spending time with her.

Sylvie was the best friend who would always be there for me, and I usually loved her company, but at the moment, I welcomed the break. Sylvie was, simply put, a bit too much at the moment, with her constant probing and need for assurance that I was okay, especially when things couldn't have been further from the truth. Thalia made conversation simple, and she had an easygoing attitude. She didn't really know me, so she didn't try see through the façade behind which I was hiding.

"How was your night with your special stranger?" she asked when we stopped to wait for a light to turn green. Her face turned briefly to regard me while her fingers kept tapping on the steering wheel to the music playing on the radio.

"It was okay, I guess." I kept my voice light as my mind searched through all the possible answers I could give. "He was nice and took me home, and that was about it."

"Nothing happened?" She turned her head to me. "Not even a kiss?" Her surprise reflected in the soft line on her forehead, but her tone remained unchanged. She had no reason to doubt me, so lying to her came easy.

I shook my head. "I kept feeling sick. Guess I had too much of Gina's favorite cocktail."

At least the first part was true.

Now was the time to ask about Gina, but for some reason I couldn't. Thalia had been such a good friend and she had helped me get a job. I couldn't afford to piss her off by accusing her friend of spiking my drink. What if hers had been spiked, too, and she knew about it all along? Instead of bringing that up, I recounted my interview with Grayson and his request that I posed nude.

"Where do you get your confidence from?" I asked when the lights changed and she hit the accelerator.

"It's really about doing what you believe in," Thalia said. "For me, confidence doesn't come with natural beauty. You can be beautiful but still not feel sexy and, hence, have no confidence. Confidence comes when you feel good about yourself and whatever you're doing. For me, that's when my hair's curled and I wear red, waterproof lipstick." She turned briefly to me and laughed out loud. "Your problem isn't that you aren't confident or sexy, Jenna. Your problem is that you try too hard to be like others. When you blend in, you become one of many and so you don't allow yourself to be unique. Maybe you should care less about what people say and do, and focus more on becoming the real you."

She grimaced and changed the radio station until she was happy with the music. Her fingers began to tap to the new rhythm almost instantly, and then she continued, "It's the only way you should be: simply *you*. Knowing that there's just one of you in the world, you should be proud of posing nude. Naturally, me being *me* is what gives me confidence."

The car slowed as we took a narrow left turn, and then

Thalia hit the accelerator with so much force I held onto my seat for support.

I swallowed the bile in my throat as I was briefly reminded of Jett's driving. He was a maniac in that department, as in so many others. He lived hard and loved harder. Relationships with men like him always come with an expiry date. It was just too bad I had to learn it the hard way.

Half an hour later, we arrived at Grayson's. Thalia locked up the car and we headed up to the studio, which, according to Thalia, had been rented out for a gallery event for the night. The guests hadn't arrived yet, which left us enough time to look around and get changed on time.

The bare walls of the studio had been transformed. Paintings and pictures in black and green hung on the walls, and tables with champagne and delicious appetizers lined the far left side, near the tall windows. I had been assured that the job would be simple. Gina, Thalia and I were instructed to dress up, then pose behind a glass wall like mannequins, and the rest of the girls had to talk and entertain guests.

I didn't mind that my green lace dress was so short that others could see all the way up to Alaska. I also didn't mind that Grayson expected me to sit still on a plush chair, with my legs on each side, so they would look longer. He had come up with the idea to cover up the fact that I was shorter than the other girls.

Wearing Thalia's black, China-doll wig, I did as instructed, keeping perfectly still. All my emotions—the good, the bad, and the worse—were hidden behind the glass, even though I felt like a mammoth stuffed in a glass house inside a museum.

By the time drinks were served, all the other models had arrived, buzzing around with excitement at the prospect of meeting new clients.

All but Gina.

I scanned the room, taking in the changes in the interior design and the unfamiliar faces, but there was no sign of her.

"Where's Gina?" I asked.

"I've no idea," Thalia said, glancing at her watch. "She's probably running late. It wouldn't be her first time."

As it turned out, Gina didn't arrive later either. A half-hour into the event, a girl with blonde curls, looking like the youngest of them all, joined us as Gina's replacement. I shot Thalia a questioning look, but there was no time for an introduction, because the actual event had started and guests were piling in.

Chapter 19

The gallery quickly filled with people. With constant new arrivals and free-flowing champagne, laughter and chatter echoed through the open space. I had never before attended a gallery event, so I had always assumed it would be a boring, apathetic experience—certainly not something full of vibrancy and life. From my heightened position, I stared at the guests, who were far less interested in the frames hanging on the walls than in socializing with the other visitors. Only a few turned their head toward the models standing behind the glass wall, paying any attention to our perfected poses. Most seemed taken in by the generous buffet, and that didn't surprise me; it looked so delicious that my stomach growled.

Half an hour turned into an hour, then two. At some point, my arms felt numb, and my smile had frozen on my lips.

"My arm's cramping," the blonde next to me mumbled, keeping her face rigid. "On top of that, I can barely feel my legs. No wonder Sarah and Gina quit on Grayson. I wouldn't bother to show up either."

Thalia suppressed a laugh, and I could certainly understand why. The blonde girl was standing, with one leg hovering over a chair, the other on the floor. Her legs were slightly trembling, and her forehead was glistening from the effort to stay impassive. I figured I had drawn the lucky straw, because I had the luxury of sitting.

For a moment, there was silence, as a group of people passed us by, their gazes glued on us before they moved on to the next distraction. The instant they were gone, the blonde let out an annoyed breath.

"He isn't usually that moody either," she said. "What's up with him?"

"What do you mean?" Thalia asked. The blonde inclined her head toward the arched doorway. I followed her line of vision and glimpsed Grayson standing next to the ugly mandrake, talking with one of his male guests, caught in some sort of disagreement, from the looks of it. His forehead was creased with either worry or annoyance, as he shook his head vehemently. We watched their heated discussion in silence.

"I tell you he's gay," the blonde said, resuming her chatter.

"Who?" Thalia asked.

"Grayson."

"Beth, you don't know that. You can't say that just because you've never seen him with a woman. Maybe he likes to keep his private life...private."

"That's my point exactly. I've never heard about him dating anyone," Beth said. "I always see him hanging around with guys, and I say that makes him gay."

Thalia rolled her eyes. "You have no clue what you're talking about."

"Fill us in then," Beth challenged. "You're into women, so maybe you should have a little chat with him. You know him better than anybody here. Maybe you can help him find his way out of the closet."

I stared at Beth in disbelief. Not that it mattered, but Thalia and Grayson were gay?

"Shut up," Thalia snapped. "Just because I've known him longer than anyone else here doesn't mean we discuss personal stuff." With an annoyed sigh, she turned her head to me. "Don't mind her," she whispered. "She's still upset that Grayson ignored her advances when she asked him out. In her book that can only mean he's playing for the other league."

"That's so last year," Beth muttered.

I stared at my employer, realizing I knew neither him nor Thalia particularly well. The day before, he had seemed quiet and reserved. Now, while he still looked impassive, there was a certain nervousness about him. He and his guest were so engrossed in whatever they were talking about that the entire room seemed to have dissolved into thin air around them. Whatever his sexual orientation was, he struck me as a strange man. I remembered the way our hands had touched. Maybe it had been a means to get my attention, but it certainly hadn't felt gay to me.

But who knew?

I wasn't an expert on the topic just because I had a few gay friends.

"Maybe this guy had the guts to tell Grayson that his mandrake is ugly, and now they're arguing about art," I suggested by ways of trying to inject a little humor into the situation and change the subject.

"Yeah." Beth laughed. "That would land him in the lions' den real quick. Grayson loves that ghastly thing."

We fell silent again, and the seconds seemed to stretch on forever. At some point, Beth let out another frustrated sigh and eventually began to stretch. "I need a smoke. If Grayson asks, tell him I had to pee."

The moment she was gone, I turned to Thalia and shot

her a smile.

"You're not going to avoid me now, are you?" she asked.

"What?" I stared at her, unsure where she was heading. "Why would I do that?"

She shrugged, as though it didn't matter, but the fleeting look in her eyes spoke volumes. "Tell me you're not one of those people who'll judge me or change your opinion of me just because I'm...different. A girl who used to work here had a huge problem with it."

I caught a strange expression on her face. It was a mixture of probing and hesitation, as if she was challenging me, testing me even. I realized there was more to the story, but I decided it best not to press the issue.

I laughed. "I'm surprised, that's all, and that's understandable, considering that we hit a straight bar yesterday, and you kept talking about the perfect guy."

"Most people assume that about me, like many other things. The moment they find out the truth, their whole attitude changes, and I become someone else in their eyes. Take my parents, for example." Thalia grimaced, and her eyes darkened with something. It wasn't anger, more like disappointment or frustration. She looked so fragile I felt sorry for her. In some way, I knew what it meant to be judged and compartmentalized.

"You don't have to worry about me." I shrugged and

left the rest unspoken. Whatever she was or wasn't, it made no difference to the fact that I saw her as a friend. "So it's true that you're into women?" I forced myself to speak the obvious, so we could move past the awkwardness of the situation.

"Yeah, but only when I have sex." Narrowing her eyes, she tilted her head to one side. "We should hook up, you know—just you and me. I know a really nice bar," she whispered. My cheeks began to burn at the insinuation.

Thalia leaned back and smiled. "I'm joking, Jenna." She let out another infectious laugh. "You should have seen your face just now. Priceless."

"I'm sorry," I mumbled. "You almost got me."

"Contrary to popular belief, we don't hit on every woman we meet," she explained. "I've been in a relationship with the same person for years, and we're still going strong."

"You're lucky then." I couldn't hide the bitter tone in my voice as I thought of Jett. "At times, I've wished to be gay, because it looks so easy. You don't seem to have all the heartbreak that comes with relationships."

She grimaced again. "Trust me, there's as much of that going on as in every other relationship. In life there might be rules. In love there are no exceptions to those rules. No one is spared from heartbreak. We all suffer it at some point or another. You simply can't control who you love and in particular, you can't control what kind of person they are."

"That's so true." I nodded in agreement, then cocked my head in curiosity. "How do you know I'm straight? I could be...anything," I asked intrigued that she could tell without really knowing me. After just one glance, she seemed to have me figured out. Was I that open a book?

"I'll be honest with you," she started. "When I saw you with your blonde friend, I wasn't sure. But by the time I picked you up from the park and Grayson wanted to talk about your work contract and his *second thoughts*, I suspected. I knew for sure at the club, when you started talking about your ex."

What second thoughts?

"What do you mean? What did Grayson say?" My glance swept over him anxiously. He was still talking with the man. Even though he wasn't looking at us, for some reason I felt as though his attention was shifting.

"Only that he could hire you for five weeks, until you're starting to show," Thalia said.

My head snapped back in her direction, and my jaw dropped. "Grayson knows?"

Thalia must have caught the shock in my voice, because she burst out in laughter.

"Of course he knows you're pregnant." She nodded mysteriously. "He's been working with women for years—

not just models, but real women. Men like him are very perceptive."

I wondered what she meant by that but didn't ask.

"No worries. I won't tell anyone or put you in an awkward position. As I said, I'm good at keeping secrets." She winked at me. "Like...I didn't tell Gina you were ordering soft drinks the entire night."

"I didn't think it was that obvious." I joined in her laughter. Now was the perfect time to ask about the drinks Gina bought. Just as I opened my mouth, Thalia shushed me.

"Look out. He's coming over."

Chapter 20

Shortly after Grayson joined our little group, the show
ended, and people began to flood out the door. Judging
from their facial expressions, some weren't pleased, if not
outraged, and the way Grayson was acting, it almost looked
like he might have actually kicked them out. I faintly
remembered Thalia telling me that we were being paid for
the night, so I'd been certain that the gallery event would
take longer than two hours. It made no sense that Grayson
had shooed his clients out so early. Something was wrong. I
could feel it. I just couldn't pinpoint what it was.

Eventually, Grayson locked up and waved us over to the
sitting area. We gathered around him in a semicircle. It was
so quiet I wouldn't have been surprised to hear a needle hit

the floor if it dropped.

"I closed the event early with good reason," Grayson said, his gaze sweeping over the inquiring faces around him. "There has been an accident, and with a heavy heart…" He paused, and for a second, I thought I heard a soft tremor in his voice. "—I deeply regret to inform you that Gina died earlier this morning."

Shock and murmur traveled through the crowd. My jaw dropped, and I clasped my hand over my mouth in disbelief. To my right, someone whimpered and began to sob.

"Oh, my God," Thalia whispered.

"What happened?" Beth asked.

Grayson linked his fingers together behind his back. His lips were drawn in a tight line, and his shoulders slumped; I almost feared his next words. "She was found on a street, stabbed, with her throat cut open," he said quietly. "The police have declared it murder."

The image of Gina lying on the street sent goosebumps up my spine.

"They think she was mugged for her handbag, because it wasn't at the crime scene when they found her at five a.m."

"Where was she found?" I didn't know why I asked the question when it didn't really matter. Everyone's head snapped in my direction. It took me every ounce of my willpower not to react when Grayson communicated the name of the street we had visited the day before. "She was attacked in a back alley, behind the La Rue bar. A bouncer found her body hidden behind a dumpster."

Another wave of shock echoed through the room, and the chatter began: gossip, I assumed. As usual, everyone had their own theory about the tragedy. As for me, my head began to spin.

"I can't believe she's dead," Thalia whispered to me. We were standing behind everyone else, with our backs to the wall. "Who would kill her and leave her lying around like trash? She was the nicest person I've ever known."

"I can't believe it either."

"And to think, we used to date before I met my current girlfriend." She shook her head in disbelief, and a tear ran down her cheek.

I turned to face her. "I'm sorry. I had no idea."

"No one did." Thalia shrugged and wiped a hand over her tear-stained face. I hugged her, because I couldn't stand seeing her in pain. It was always sad when someone died. As short as my meeting with Gina had been, and in spite of the questionable drinks, I had still liked her as a person.

Her death was such a tragedy, and it had come out of the blue. It felt surreal to know we had seen her less than twenty-four hours ago; my memories of the redhead were still fresh in my mind.

"She must have gone back to the La Rue bar," Thalia

whispered.

My attention snapped in her direction. "What do you mean? Why would she do that?"

"After you hooked up with that guy, Gina and I had one more drink together. I got a headache and called it a day, but she decided to stay, so I left, figuring she'd be all right," she said, barely able hide her remorse. "I should have stayed. Maybe this wouldn't have happened. Maybe she'd still be alive."

Or maybe they'd both be dead.

"Did she meet anyone else?" I asked, keeping my true thoughts to myself.

But Thalia didn't hear me anymore; she simply walked away mumbling, "I have to tell him."

I followed her and stopped a step behind, listening to her conversation with Grayson.

"Jenna, Gina and I visited the La Rue bar yesterday," she said. Silence fell over the room as everyone turned to look at her. "We had a few drinks together before we moved on to the HUSH HUSH club. That was the last place we saw her."

Grayson's face remained an impenetrable mask. "Just the three of you?" he asked, and Thalia nodded.

His forehead creased into a frown as his gaze swept over the shocked faces around him, then settled on Thalia's again. Finally, he turned. Following his line of vision, I realized the guy he had been talking to before hadn't left with the rest of the guests. He was standing in the background, near the wall, hidden in the shadows, observing us all along.

I frowned.

"I'd like to introduce you to Detective Barrow," Grayson said grimly. "He's leading the investigation."

As the man stepped forward, my heart spluttered in my chest and skipped a beat.

Oh, my God.

Oh. My. God.

It was in that instant that I recognized him as the guy from the hotel. The guy with the newspaper. The guy who had glanced at me. My breath remained trapped in my throat, and my knees began to shake, threatening to buckle beneath me.

What was he doing here?

"I'm afraid I'll have to keep you girls a little longer," I heard Grayson say. "Detective Barrow will want to ask each of you a few questions, but no worries. In spite of the disruption in our work schedule, you'll still be paid your usual fee for the night. Feel free to leave after the detective's done with you. Any questions?"

I shook my head, but not because I didn't have any questions.

My heart pounded in my chest, and my blood rushed

hard as I stared at the man from the hotel, my mind circling around one single thought.

What are the odds?

End of episode 2

Jett and Brooke's story continues in the powerfully sensual next part in the No Exceptions series,

THE

LOVER'S

PROMISE

COMING OCTOBER 2014!

Never miss a release. Use the chance to request Jett's POV or get a sneak peek, teasers, or win amazing prizes, such as an e-reader of your choice, gift cards, and ARCs by signing up to my newsletter.

As a subscriber, you'll also receive an email reminder on release day:

http://www.jcreedauthor.blogspot.com/p/mailing-list.html

THE LOVER'S PROMISE (NO EXCEPTIONS BOOK 3) SNEAK PEEK

CHAPTER 1

Calm down.

Calm the fuck down.

There was nothing to fear, because I had done nothing wrong. It had been Gina's idea to visit the club, not mine. All I had to do was answer the detective's questions and then I was free to leave.

Countless thoughts raced through my head but only one registered: Gina was dead. Killed. Who would have done it? And for a handbag? Even as I asked myself those questions, I knew a mugging wasn't the answer. While people stole handbags, they didn't necessarily cut the victim's throat in the process, which was why the detective was here—to unravel the mystery and get to the bottom of things. Like me, he probably suspected foul play and while I hoped he'd find the killer, I also hoped that, just because Thalia and I happed to be the last people who saw Gina alive, we wouldn't end up as persons of interest.

"Jenna?" Grayson's voice drew me back to reality. "You're the first. The detective would like to ask you a few questions now."

Oh, shit.

The icy knot in my stomach intensified, growing as big as an iceberg under the water's surface. Why did I have to go first when I didn't want to? He'd only pour all his energy into grilling me, and I had no answers, no clues, nothing to help out in any way.

Basically, I was doomed to look like I was guilty.

"Great. I'll be happy to help," I said weakly and shot Grayson a confident smile, avoiding the detective's intense stare. To be honest, I had no idea if he remembered our brief encounters at the hotel, but I could feel his gaze burning a hole in my head. When I finally dared look up, I realized his eyes not only rested on me, but there was also a flicker of recognition clearly written on his face. I froze in horror.

This is what happens when you stare at a guy you don't know, Stewart. You come across as a complete creep.

Back then, I had probably looked like a guilty mess to him. I swallowed down the lump in my throat, and tried to behave as innocently as possible.

"Detective, you're welcome to use my office," Grayson

said, oblivious to my frayed nerves.

"Thank you. It won't take long," the man said while his stare remained glued to me.

Please, don't leave me alone with him.

I felt like a lamb scheduled to be slaughtered. My skin began to itch from the strain of trying to act casual. I had done nothing wrong, and yet his intense glance made me feely guilty. Talk about unfair. Talk about the crappiest day of my life. The crappiest of all crappy days.

The detective turned on his heels and motioned me to follow him, and so I did, unsure what would happen next. To the daunting sound of impending doom, we walked into Grayson's office. I was like that woman in white, ready to be sacrificed to King Kong and could almost hear the proverbial drums beating in the background. I felt completely paralyzed with fear. With my heart pounding hard against my chest, I took a seat and waited for the detective to do the same.

He didn't sit down, which was probably a ruse to infuse respect into a suspect. He wasn't even *that* tall, so under normal circumstances he wouldn't have intimidated me. But there was nothing normal about today.

I peered around me, considering getting out of Grayson's office by faking fainting. I had always wanted to do that, and figured that was the perfect moment, if only to avoid the probing questions and mistrust that would follow.

I took a deep breath and let it out slowly, then closed my eyes for a moment, envisioning the scene. Just too bad I wasn't cut out for acting. In my head, I promised myself that I'd sign up for some much-needed acting classes. That is, if I ever made it out of here and saved up enough money.

The detective turned the knob and closed the door behind him.

Now, we were alone.

Just he and I—behind a closed door.

Dum. Dum Dum.

No, make that doom. Doom—as the imaginary drums continued to pound in my head.

My whole body began to shake slightly as he slid into Grayson's seat and pulled out a notepad from his pocket. The whole situation felt surreal, like I was starring in a horror movie. I almost expected him to retrieve a string of rope and tie up my wrists to the chair, maybe even switch on a neon lamp, or hang me upside down to torture me into giving him the answers he wanted.

Only, I had no answers.

Let the witch hunt begin.

Sighing, I crossed my arms over my chest, ready to face whatever the detective would throw at me.

He glanced around the room and his eyes came to rest on the model pictures on the wall. Grayson's glory. The gems he'd shaped into diamonds—as he liked to proclaim. Every one of his models was up there; everyone but me. It wasn't that much of a surprise, given that I was new and had yet to book a job. A short silence ensued, during which Detective Barrow assessed me, his right hand stroking his neck in a strange manner. I twitched uncomfortably in my chair and crossed my legs, waiting, assessing him back.

"So, Mr. Grayson told me you joined two days ago. Is that correct?" he started eventually.

"Yes." I nodded, staring at him blankly and gradually relaxed, happy that he didn't ask about the hotel. Maybe he didn't remember me after all. Maybe it was just a normal investigation and his frown came as a part of the job description, meaning it had nothing to do with me personally.

"All right." He smiled politely and opened his notepad. "Let's start with the last time you saw Gina alive and we'll take it from there. You mentioned you went out?"

It wasn't a question, but rather a statement. I had mentioned no such thing to him.

I nodded. "After Grayson offered me a trial period to see whether I was cut out for the job, Thalia invited me and Gina for a drink at the La Rue Bar. We had a few drinks, then Gina suggested we visit the Hush Hush bar, and we had some more drinks there."

God, why did it sound like I was a complete party girl

when it couldn't be further from the truth?

The detective nodded and scribbled a few words on his notepad without looking up. "What happened after?"

"Gina tried to hook me up with a guy." *Cringe.* I didn't need to hear the detective's thoughts; I could *read* them from his expression and they weren't pretty. I brushed my hair out of my face and continued. "I started to feel sick so a guy brought me home. And that was the last time I saw her."

I recounted the same story I had told Thalia: That a stranger drove me home, and then left. "Thalia said she had one last drink with Gina after I left. What happened after that, I don't know. You'll have to ask her."

"The man who drove you home—" He stopped scribbling and looked up from his pad, his eyes the color of brown parchment assessing me. "—what did you say his name was?"

"I don't remember," I lied. "I was too drunk."

The detective pressed his lips in a tight line. The way he was drumming his fingers on the table made me nervous, so I looked away, mentally counting the seconds until I could get the hell out.

"Did anything strange happen yesterday? Such as a fight, not necessarily between you and the victim?" I shook my head and he continued, "Can you think of anyone who might have held a grudge against her?"

A new spasm of nerves coursed through me.

"No, of course not." I brushed my hair out of my face as I considered my words carefully. "I only just met her so didn't know her particularly well, but it seemed Gina is…was friendly with all the girls here. I think everyone liked her."

"How was the relationship between Gina and Thalia?"

I paused taken aback by the strange question. "Good, I guess. I think they were good friends. Like I said, I only met them both recently."

"If anything unusual happened, no matter how trivial you think it might be, I need you to tell me. It's the little things that often carry enough weight to break a case. Do you understand?" He stared at me. "They're often relevant."

His tone worried me.

"I wish I could be of more help, but I don't remember much, except that Gina brought us drinks," I said carefully. "We got drunk. We had fun. And the next thing I knew a guy drove me home."

Even though I omitted quite a bit, I stuck to the truth. My mind had been a blurry mess. Yesterday's events seemed so far away, they almost resembled a dream. The only thing I remembered was the way Jett had broken my fall, and the fake name he had given me, but I couldn't share that with the detective. For some inexplicable reason,

I couldn't tell anyone about the Jett incident. It was like my brain wanted to lock that episode away forever.

When I finally finished my recounting, the detective opened a folder on the table. "Maybe these pictures will jolt your memory." Slowly, he began to sort through countless sheets of paper and pictures.

"Did Gina wear this make up when you last saw her?" He slid over the first picture and I shrank back in shock.

It was a headshot of Gina. For a second, it looked like she was sleeping, until I registered that her eyes were slightly open, and a dried trail of blood marked her chin. There was no doubt the picture had been taken after her death and the discovery of her body. The rest of her body from the neck wasn't on the picture. If there were, I knew I would have needed therapy for the next few years.

"What do you mean?" I asked slowly. Her face and lips were so pale they almost had a blue shimmer to them. I had never seen a corpse in real life, not even when my father and my sister died.

The detective pointed his finger to her left cheek. "Did she have the two spots on her face?"

I narrowed my eyes in concentration and finally grasped the meaning of his words. There were two dots on her cheek—like two little moles or freckles. Come to think of it, they didn't really stand out. They had been painted onto the skin in a fashionable but such a realistic way, that it wasn't glaringly obvious that they weren't real.

"No, " I said and shook my head. "Not as far as I remember."

He nodded, as if my answer confirmed his suspicion, and handed me the second picture.

"Do you recognize this man?" he asked.

I looked from the detective to the picture, and my heart froze.

Holy mother of grace.

That couldn't be possible. I blinked several times as an array of emotions washed over me.

Staring back at me was Jett's face.

End of sample

To those, who want to learn more about Brooke's past
and the story behind the Lucazzone estate, I welcome
you to read the prequel of No Exceptions:

SURRENDER
YOUR LOVE
J.C.REED

A THANK YOU LETTER

There are so many things I want to say at the end of a book, but in the end it all comes down to six words:

THANK YOU for reading my books!

Writing this book was a dream come true as was fleshing out the characters that haunted me even in my deepest dreams, urging me to tell their story.

I hope you were entertained and enjoyed reading it as much as I enjoyed writing it. If you can take out some time, please leave a review on amazon.com, barnesandnoble.com, iTunes, or Goodreads, or simply write me. And please call me Jessica. I noticed a lot of readers start with "hello," and I get why. You're not sure if you should call me J. or J.C. Let me settle this for you. Call me by my first name. And when you write, please know I always write back.

I look forward to hearing from you! I'm forever grateful and hope you will enjoy my next release.

Jessica C. Reed

ACKNOWLEDGMENTS

First and foremost, thank you, Shannon Wolfman, for being the best friend and critique partner any author can have. You have never let me down. Never. Not one single time. Even if I'm close to giving up, deleting chapters and killing off characters, you're the one who pushes me to get going, reminding me that every story has to be told. Thank you for forcing me to sit down and write those hot scenes and then pointing out all the weird things I wrote when my brain decided to switch off for a while.

I won't forget the laughs we shared or the fact that you always go above and beyond the call of duty and friendship. You're fucking amazing. If there was an award, it would go to you for being the best friend ever.

I want to thank the wonderful bloggers who started the journey with me and never let me down. Thank you for fitting me into your busy schedule and for always being there. I love you all.

Thank you to my freaking awesome agent Lauren E. Abramo for pitching my work and answering countless of annoying questions. You rock!

Thank you to my editors and cover artist for their hard work. You never fail to amaze me.

Thank you to my little munchkins for understanding that mommy's busy writing a book in the late hours of the night. And no, sorry, I can't read my books aloud as a bedtime story, but maybe later when you're older (which I hope you'll never be.)

And, finally, I want to thank God for allowing me to meet the best readers I can have.

Connect with me online:

http://www.jcreedauthor.blogspot.com

http://www.facebook.com/pages/JC-Reed/295864860535849

http://www.twitter.com/jcreedauthor

42873987R00145

Made in the USA
Lexington, KY
08 July 2015